Inspector Proby's Christmas

Inspector Proby's Christmas

John Gano

St. Martin's Press
New York

Library of Congress Cataloging-in-Publication Data

Gano, John.
    Inspector Proby's Christmas / John Gano.
        p.   cm.
    ISBN 0-312-11292-0
    I. Title.
PR6057.A47I57   1994
823'.914—dc20   94-32249
                                                                    CIP

First published in Great Britain by Macmillan London Limited

First U.S. Edition: December 1994
10 9 8 7 6 5 4 3 2 1

Inspector Proby's Christmas

Prologue

In the little shop a couple were holding hands and gazing down at the open case of brooches lying on the counter. The man picked one up and held it against his companion's throat. She smiled up at him and, turning to the shopkeeper, he said something that made the other man grin.

None of them noticed a figure, wrapped in a white mackintosh and holding a paper bag, watching them with great concentration from beneath the pink and white awning of a butcher's shop across the narrow street. It was raining slightly – summer rain that softens the air and spatters your face with its light refreshing touch.

The jeweller, a pale chubby man with bright rosy cheeks and thick opaque spectacles, produced a red box into which the enamel they had chosen was carefully placed. He handed the box to the man who, in turn, passed it on to his companion with a slightly self-conscious flourish. She gave a little bob and in the street, the watcher's fingers clenched in a convulsive spasm that shattered the contents of the bag, sending little slivers of glass pattering on to the cobbles. Blood ran through the fingers – a bright thick red stream flowing steadily from the deep cut, spilling unnoticed down the raincoat, as the watcher's eyes filled with tears.

When the couple came laughing out of the little shop, there was no one in the street, and the droning and hooting of the market day's bustle drowned the sound of other footsteps running haywire down a side alley out of sight.

1

Chapter 1

'Are you awake?'

Jim Proby rolled over with a groan and hid his rumpled face beneath a pillow. He felt his wife's hand shaking his shoulder with irritating persistence.

'Are you awake?' Her voice was muffled, as if coming down a long tunnel.

'What time is it?' he murmured.

'It's Rootham. He wants to speak to you. He sat up, blinked in the scalding light, and took the receiver – a tall man, with curly grey hair, impressive even in his baggy striped pyjamas.

'Yes? What? I see!'

His wife, thin-lipped, dropped her feet into her slippers and reached for her dressing gown.

'I'll make the tea,' she said, as he listened to his sergeant's instructions.

'Pick me up in fifteen minutes.' He coughed convulsively and hung up. Reaching for his wristwatch, he glumly noted the time: 3.18. And they hadn't got to bed till after midnight.

'Are you the only policeman in Hampton?' asked his wife sourly as he gulped down the tea.

'Don't be like that, Sheila.' He took her long pale hand and squeezed it. 'Some poor woman's been done in by the canal. You'd want me to catch the bastard.' With his dark eyes, ready smile and sharp inquisitive nose, he radiated a kindly strength.

She smiled, her pretty face enlivened by an answering warmth.

2

They heard a car draw up, and steps coming up to the door.

'I don't know why Rootham doesn't just live here,' she said. 'It would save all this telephoning.'

He laughed, putting on his jacket.

'Have you got your gloves?' she asked, suddenly solicitous. 'There's a frost, remember.'

'I remember.' He bent down and kissed her mouth. 'See you.'

'See you.' She caught his arm. 'Be careful.'

'What have you got?'

Detective Sergeant Rootham steered the car out of the drowsy suburb and accelerated down the slip road on to the motorway. The frosted trees shone in the headlights, and there was still a slight haze left over from the fog that rolled nightly up from the broad river below.

'Young woman. Fully clothed. No sign of interference. Head blown in. Shotgun. Two shots heard by the lock-keeper. That's about it. The doctor's on his way. It's just down here.'

They had turned off at the first exit and already Jim could see the insistent flicker of other blue lights through the trees beyond the warehouse.

'What do you reckon?' He was looking down at what had once been a woman. The body was just fine, but the face was stripped away, revealing splintered bone and much more that he would have preferred not to see.

'I'll tell you more after the autopsy.' Dr Milligan the police surgeon was an old friend, and each knew how the other was feeling. 'Funny thing though. I reckon the second shot was fired after she was dead.'

Jim knelt down and examined her hands. They were chilled by the frost, but still palpable. The nails were painted a soft pink, and she was wearing a wedding ring.

'Anyone got a torch?'

One of the uniformed constables, who was stretching tape across the towpath, came over.

'There you are, sir.'

'Shine it here, would you?' He had taken off the ring and was peering at the inscription.

'To D from J. Always.' And then the date.

'Thanks,' he said. 'I want a list of contents as soon as possible.' He walked back and sat down wearily in the passenger seat.

'Reckon he was trying to prevent identification?' Rootham asked when he came back from supervising the preliminary ground search. Jim shook his head.

'If so, he did a bloody bad job,' he replied. 'She won't be hard to trace. She was married last week.' And he bent forward and rested his head on the dashboard.

'Christ!'

'Poor kid,' said Jim as the ambulance pulled away in front of them, the driver winking at Rootham as he passed. 'Let's get back and set this job up.'

Chapter 2

'You heard the shots?'

The lock-keeper, a hefty man with a dark face blurred by three days' silver stubble, nodded.

'I said so, didn't I?' His voice was tired but aggressive. 'First one shot . . . startled the life out of me . . . and then a second – one – no, two minutes later. How many more times do I have to tell you?'

'We need to get the details straight,' said Proby in a soothing voice.

'Or don't you want to help us?' sneered Rootham, leaning forward menacingly.

'Oh yes,' said the man. 'Likely I'd want some crazed bugger with a shotgun marching up and down outside my home!'

'It's six years since your last little trouble,' murmured Proby, leafing through some papers. The man dropped his eyes.

'I got off, didn't I?' he whined. 'There's no call to bring that up again.'

'No, no,' said Proby. 'But others will. That's why it's in your interest to give us all you can.'

'Look,' said the dishevelled man, 'what more can I tell you? There were two shots, like I've said. I went out in my pullover to see what was up. I slipped in the poor girl's blood and I went up to Margetson's to ring for you lot. Bloody hell!' he suddenly shouted. 'If I'd tipped her into the bleeding canal with a couple of those boulders you'd have been none the wiser. I reckon that's what

5

he'd 'ave done, if I hadn't disturbed him.' He stopped suddenly.

'So you saw him?' snapped Rootham. 'You saw the murderer and you haven't told us?' He made a move towards the man which Proby restrained.

'Hold off, Ted. I'm sure Willie just forgot. Now,' he went on, standing up and bending over the lock-keeper, 'tell us about him.'

'I didn't see him,' muttered Willie mutinously. 'I've told you that, but I did hear something. Footsteps – or rather just one. It gave me a real turn. First the body and then this sound. I just ran, I can tell you.'

'Is this yours?' Proby slid a plastic bag across the table. It contained a small red enamel pocket-knife, with a blade open but half snapped off. The man glared at it, obviously at a loss for words.

'Is it yours?' shouted Rootham. 'Yes or no?'

If the man wanted to deny it, it was too late. He nodded sullenly. 'Yes,' he said. 'That's mine. What of it?'

'We found it in the long grass behind the willows.'

The man shrugged. 'I might have dropped it any time,' he said. 'It's been missing a week or so.'

'Tell us more about the footstep, Willie,' said Proby. 'Where do you reckon it came from?'

The man thought. 'It was somewhere in front of me,' he said. 'I was kneeling in all that mess. Then I heard it.' He paused. 'Do you know . . . I reckon he was behind that old wooden shed, the one Gaffer Trent used to keep his tackle in. Yes!' His eyes opened wider with the dawning thought. 'That's where he must have been. I reckon I was lucky. I must have gone right past him up to Margetson's.'

After he had left, the two detectives looked at each other.

'Pity about the pen-knife,' said Rootham. 'I had that down to the murderer.'

'Mmm.' Proby shrugged. 'He was right about the shed.' He pulled out a carefully drawn site plan which had already been prepared for them. 'See? If you'd heard

6

someone coming up the towpath, you've only got two places to hide: there or behind the trees.'

'It makes that matchstick potentially interesting.'

'Yeah. Pity about the frost. Yes?' This to a tap at the door which opened to reveal a young policewoman, the severe uniform altogether failing to disguise her youthful allure.

'I've got the contents list and the scene-of-crime report,' she announced. 'The medical report will be another half-hour. Dr Milligan's assistant rang us to say she'd bring it over herself.'

'Fine. Thank you, Julie.'

'Like some coffee?'

'Yes, please, and our electronics engineer.'

'What's wrong now?' She laughed, coming further into the room. She had fair hair, cut in a short bob, and round blue eyes beneath delicately curved brows.

'This computer terminal,' grumbled Proby, stabbing at the keyboard with his forefinger. 'I can't make the silly thing connect into the Rookforce program at High Wycombe. That's the second time this week.'

'Let me.' She sat down, flicked a couple of buttons, stared at the screen and laughed again. 'Well, of course you can't,' she said. 'You've got it hooked into Belfast.' Her fingers rattled over the keys. 'There you are,' she said, 'Rookforce. What's your code?'

'179G,' he said. Smiling she keyed it in and the first of the questionnaires designed to cross-check the details of all mainland violent crime filled the screen.

'Away you go.' She stood up. 'I'll go and make the coffee. Black, two sugars and white with none.'

The two men nodded gratefully.

'It's lucky I know my place,' she laughed. 'I don't know what you'd do without me.'

Both men watched her leave with undisguised admiration.

'It'll be a blow when she gets promotion,' said Rootham.

Proby grinned. 'Well, get ready,' he said. 'Because I

signed the recommendation last week. She's a smart girl. She's too good for us.'

'Speak for yourself,' replied Rootham, adding 'sir' as the divisional Chief Superintendent poked his face round the door.

'Any news re the girl, Jim?'

Proby stood up politely to face the older man, a soldierly figure with a rough good-humoured face.

'Nothing yet, sir. Premeditated, I would say, and not sexual. We're trying to trace her identity at the moment.'

The Superintendent grunted. 'Right! But keep me in close touch. This may make the nationals.'

'Yes, sir.' The door closed.

They studied the contents file. She had been wearing new jeans and a thick blue fisherman's jersey with the label of a local shop. Her thick socks were handknitted and the heavy walking boots came from a London store. Apart from the wedding ring, there had been no jewellery. In one pocket she had had a small handkerchief, two contraceptives, a fresh piece of chewing gum and two five-pound notes. In the other pocket she had an empty packet of Disprin, an old cinema ticket stub and a pound coin. Nothing more.

'That's funny,' said Proby.

'You mean no torch?'

'Yes. There was no moon. Willie didn't even see her till he fell over her. How did she get there? She didn't even have a cigarette lighter. Who's checking the church registers?'

'Allan and Braithwaite. Hickock's trawling the divisional computer log and Oates is checking with missing persons.' The two men fell silent, Proby continuing to punch the preliminary details into the computer while Rootham watched him, longing for a cigarette but not quite daring to ask.

'Go on,' said Proby. 'Go and smoke one outside, I've got plenty on my hands with this contraption for the next few minutes.'

8

And then, in quick succession, things began to happen. First Julie brought in their coffee, strong aromatic coffee she had brewed herself rather than the smoky fluid discharged by the office machine. Immediately behind her came Mrs Grant from the laboratory with the medical report. And before Proby could do more than lift the welcome mug, Braithwaite, the youngest man on their team, straight off the beat, with eager eyes and a wisp of a moustache, charged in shouting, 'I've found her, guv. Found her straight off!'

'All right. All right.' Proby put down his coffee in deference to the young man's eagerness. 'Let's hear it.'

'Well,' the young man opened his notebook. 'Something about her suggested a classy background. I mean, she looked sort of well cared for, didn't she?' The others just listened. 'So, I got to thinking. She must have been attractive, I mean, with a figure like that, cheaply dressed but smart like. So I thought maybe the old town. Like those girls who swan around where the artists work.'

'Come on,' said Rootham, fidgeting with his cigarette packet, 'don't keep us in suspense!'

'So I went to All Saints Church, and the vicar described her exactly, and the initials fit. Must be the same. And get this. The geezer she married was Hippo Doyle!'

If he had hoped for a sensation, he wasn't disappointed.

'Hippo Doyle!' repeated Proby, as Rootham let out a long low whistle. 'That brings back a few memories.'

'But he must be forty or more,' put in Julie. 'And he's only been out six months.'

'He was always a smooth worker, was Hippo,' said Proby. 'Well done,' he added to the young detective. 'That was good work. Get Hippo's address – he'll be registered with the Queen Street station – while I just have a look at the medical report. Get it down on paper and bring it straight back here.'

Mrs Grant, who had been standing patiently behind Julie, came over to his desk.

'Dr Milligan said to give him a ring if you want more

9

detail. He thought this would serve to get you started.'

'Thanks,' he said and she hurried off, a trim woman with prematurely greying hair.

'Here, have a look.' Rootham and Julie peered over his shoulder as they read the report together. It was quite straightforward. Death had been instantaneous, caused by a massive trauma to the brain. The second shot had been discharged into the head after death. Her age was estimated at between eighteen and twenty-five, she was in excellent health, her last meal had been eaten three hours before death and had consisted of a hamburger and ice cream. She was also three months pregnant.

The size of shot used was a No. 6, standard to sporting cartridges, and the gun had been discharged not more than four yards from her for both shots. He estimated the time of death at between midnight and 2 a.m. At the bottom of the report he had scribbled as an afterthought: 'I think she might have been in the habit of taking cocaine.'

Braithwaite's report named the girl as Diana Mary Smyth of 33, Jew's Hill, Hampton, parents both deceased, lately married to John Percy Doyle of 94, The Avenue. Hampton was a hybrid town, containing one third industrial wasteland round the disused docks, one third old cathedral city and one third modern suburbs. If Jew's Hill was one of the more decorative medieval streets, The Avenue was certainly the roughest among the wasteland, a winding road littered with half-abandoned cars.

No. 94 was an unappetizing villa, set back from the road, in the shadow of the gas works.

They took two cars, just in case. Braithwaite and Allan watched the back, while Proby walked up to the front door, one hand casually clasping the newly issued revolver in his pocket. Rootham, with a second gun, was at the corner of the street. Proby rang the bell. It was opened immediately by an immense man, wearing nothing but a bath towel knotted underneath his belly. He was wearing

10

a wedding ring identical to the one in Proby's pocket.

'Morning, Hippo!' said Proby, his finger curling involuntarily towards the trigger of his gun. 'Been taking a bath?'

'Good morning, Detective Inspector,' replied the other in a voice that surprised by being both courteous and quiet. 'I hardly expected to see you here.'

'Can I come in?'

'Not if you're going to shoot me with that toy in your pocket. These must be your friends playing cowboys and Indians in my back garden.' The big man smiled. 'And I do believe that's Sergeant Rootham hiding behind a lamp-post. What am I supposed to have done now?'

'Let me come in, Hippo,' said Proby. 'I'm sure you're too sensible to do anything stupid.'

The big man opened the door wide. 'Be my guest.'

In sharp contrast to the ugly exterior, inside the house was welcoming and colourful. The lounge was crammed with imitation French furniture, in the Louis Quinze style, all serpentine legs and shiny pink silk. Over the fireplace hung a huge framed photograph of a young woman, smiling provocatively in a tight lace dress.

'You haven't met my missus,' said Hippo. 'Fancy a drink?'

Proby sat down heavily, shaking his head. 'Is she here?' he asked in a neutral tone.

Hippo frowned. 'What's that to you?'

'Is she here?' Proby asked again. There was a footfall upstairs and both men looked up at the ceiling.

'What if she is?'

Proby sighed. It never was easy, dealing with people who expected you to disrupt their lives, whether with good reason or not.

'There's a young girl been found dead by the canal,' he said. 'We thought it might be her.' The giant's face changed slowly from truculence through suspicious uncertainty to obvious alarm.

'Dead? My Didie?' He seized Proby's arm. 'Why do you think it's her?' He bared his black uneven teeth in a

11

grimace. 'If it is, I'll fucking top the man who did it. Not Didie!'

Proby had taken out the wedding ring. Now he put it on the table, with an apologetic look into the other man's eyes. There were more footsteps upstairs and then a woman's voice calling, 'Hippo! Where are you?'

The big man crossed to the door. 'Get your clothes and go home, Hannah.' And yet it was still said in his quiet, polite voice.

'Is that the wedding ring?' Proby's voice betrayed nothing beyond a desire for information. Twenty years as a police officer had taught him to accept other people's lives, in all their variety, without judging them. Hippo picked it up and slid it on to his little finger. 'Yes.' There were tears in his eyes. 'I worshipped her. That's why I let her sleep around. It was her nature, you see. Like a wild animal.'

'Mind if we search the house?'

'You go right ahead. I'll come down the station now. I know you'll want a statement.'

Proby gestured at the telephone. 'Do you want Mr Gilston to come?'

Hippo shook his head. 'Why waste good money?' he said. 'I know you'll treat me fair. This is one villain I want you to catch. Once you put him inside, he's mine.'

Chapter 3

'Well of course he did it.' Sheila Proby was heaping stew on to her husband's plate while the Roothams watched her greedily. 'Hippo Doyle! You've always said he was the most violent man north of Watford.'

'What I want to know,' said Mollie Rootham, a mousy little woman in a mini skirt, 'is why he's at large at all. You've done him twice for robbery with violence and once for manslaughter. Why don't they just throw away the key?' The others laughed. It was part of their shared mythology that Mollie was the hanger and flogger of the group.

'He's an educated man, isn't he?' asked Rootham. 'Oxbridge – that sort of thing.'

'Yes.' Jim Proby's mouth was full of lamb. 'He got a first at Balliol. Studying Classics.'

'He must be on parole,' said Sheila. 'What did you find in his house?'

'Nothing material,' lied Proby, who didn't want to discuss his latest lead. 'But thanks to Dr Milligan we did find enough cocaine to put Hippo back in Brixton if we need to. Personally I think it was the girl's private cache. But it might come in handy for a holding charge.'

After dinner they settled down to their weekly game of Scrabble, parting with much laughter at their traditional hour of eleven o'clock. Both men rose early, and both were in the mood for love.

'I've hardly seen you this week,' grumbled Sheila drowsily as she lay curled up in his arms in the half-light from the street lamp.

13

'But I'm here now,' he said patiently, stroking her back and breathing in the scent of her damp hair.

'I can't think why I married a policeman,' she murmured, but already she was half asleep as he lay awake longingly watching the rise and fall of her breasts.

What he had found, hidden in Mrs Doyle's laundry bag, was a small pile of letters, recently dated. Their contents left no doubt as to the relationship with the man who signed himself 'S'. Each letter detailed his elaborate intentions for their next tryst together with some self-satisfied comments on past encounters. If Hippo had found them, they were more than sufficient to establish motive. But there were three snags. The first was that Hippo had an alibi from his wife's sister with whom he had spent the whole night. The second was that he had passed the paraffin test for firearms. And the third was that Proby didn't for a moment believe he had done it. Against him, Hippo had an unappetizing record of savage violence, usually with a pickaxe though never once involving firearms. But towards women, he was well known to be scrupulous not to say old-fashioned in his courtesy. He might, would even, have disembowelled 'S' in the middle of Marks and Spencers if necessary, but the sadistic private murder of his wife was right out of his territory. This was what also kept Proby awake, as, all around him, the smart executive houses in the suburbs of Hampton sheltered their sleeping inhabitants from the freezing December fog.

Down among the deserted warehouses by the docks, Mary Grogan listened to the echo of her heels as she turned past the old customs shed and started up the steps towards the Anchor Inn. She was a short girl, with a freckled nose, her pretty face framed by thick reddish curls.

A hundred years before, Hampton had been a major port, with a constant stream of ships trading in and out of the river mouth, their sailors swapping cheerful banter with the little fishing fleet that bobbed up and down the coast in search of herring. There were scarcely two weeks

14

to go before Christmas and she was carrying a wicker basket full of knitted sweaters collected from her grandmother for family distribution. Suddenly she noticed a change in the pattern of sound. She stopped. Silence. And yet she was sure she had heard a separate footstep echoing her own brisk clatter. She gripped the handrail and nerved herself to look backwards. There was no one there. The wisps of river mist drifted easily past the menacing buildings, illuminated only by a couple of sodium lights on the nearest warehouse, the only one still in regular use. In between the angles of those empty emblems of the port's decline, she could just make out the glitter of her grandmother's porch light, from the old harbourmaster's house. She shivered and started to climb again. In five minutes she would be inside the Anchor, with its welcome stench of sweat and half-digested beer. She tossed her head with ironic disdain and stifled a little cry as a pale figure appeared at the top of the steps. She opened her mouth to speak, but no sound would come. The figure was carrying something, pointing something: she dropped her basket to raise an arm – half in supplication, half in self-defence. There was a flash of flame as she felt herself thrown backwards by a stunning winding blow, even before she dimly heard the explosion, followed by another flash, and nothing.

'Will she live?' Proby, summoned again from his bed, was hurrying down the corridor to keep pace with the surgeon. The latter, a thin man with dark smudges under his eyes, stopped abruptly. His white tunic and bare hairless arms were stained with blood.

'I don't know,' he said. 'Personally, I doubt it. But we're doing everything we can. Now I have to attend to another patient.' The alarm clipped to his lapel started vibrating noisily again, and he set off at a trot, leaving Proby to walk slowly back again to the double doors of the operating theatre. Rootham and Hickock were waiting for him with a plastic cup filled with steaming cocoa.

'Any news?'

They both shook their heads, Hickock's heavy jowls wobbling lugubriously. Proby sat down beside them in the row of battered plastic chairs. A nurse, fully masked, came out and, ignoring them, went over to the vending machine. She slid in a coin and pressed a button. Nothing happened. Unexpectedly she aimed a heavy kick at the machine. It clattered in protest.

'Bloody hell!' she muttered and walked back past them into the theatre. Before the door swung shut behind her, they caught a glimpse of something lying on a stretcher surrounded by a plastic curtain. There was a thin vibration of infinitesimal sounds, the whisper of a fan, the subdued staccato beeps of electronic machinery. Somewhere behind them they heard a door open, then the sound, instantly suppressed, of a voice. Looking down the long corridor, with its walls divided horizontally – dark green to waist level, a dull cream above – they saw a little group of people walking slowly towards them. A tiny woman had her head buried in the breast of a tall bulky man, his dark eyes staring straight ahead, one arm fixed supportively round the woman's shoulders. Beside them was Detective Constable Braithwaite looking absurdly young in a short camel-hair overcoat. Julie, crisply uniformed, brought up the rear, whispering in an undertone to a pale young man who was mopping his eyes with a handkerchief.

Proby made himself stand up and walk towards them.

'Mr and Mrs Grogan?'

The man nodded. 'Are you the doctor, then?' he asked in a husky undertone.

'No,' said Proby. 'I'm Detective Inspector Proby. I'm in charge of the investigation.'

'Where's the doctor, then?' said the man, staring at Rootham and Hickock. 'He's the man I want to see.'

'Tea or coffee?' asked Julie. The man shook his head, steering his wife to Proby's chair and settling down beside her.

16

'We just want to see our Mary,' he said gruffly.

'I'd like to ask you a few questions,' said Proby. 'I realize that this is a dreadful moment for both of you. But I need some details. I'm sure you understand.'

The man shrugged. 'What can I tell you? A lovelier lass never lived. There's nobody would wish her harm.' His wife's body shook with sobs. The young man turned away, raising his eyes to read the sign over the theatre door.

'How old is Mary?' asked Proby, stumbling over the words as he realized he had nearly used the past tense.

'She's seventeen,' said her father. 'She'll be eighteen next May.'

'Is she still at school?'

'Oh aye!' he said. 'Hampton High School. In Abbey Street.'

Rootham had begun to take notes. 'Does she have a boyfriend?'

The man glowered at him. 'If you'd call him that.'

'His name?'

'Jeff Hines. He lives in Bedington. His dad's got the garage on the bypass.'

'Do you know the address?'

'Jeff wouldn't have done this,' interrupted the little woman fiercely. 'This is some maniac.' She started crying again and the man put both arms round her and hugged her to him closely. The surgeon came back down the corridor. He was wearing a fresh overall and had washed his arms. His short green rubber boots squeaked on the shiny floor.

'Mr Grogan?' While he talked to the girl's family, Proby sent Rootham back to the dockyard to report on progress, while Braithwaite and Hickock left together, one to interview the boyfriend, the other to check on Hippo Doyle.

After a while he managed to get the surgeon aside.

'I've got to ask you this,' he said.

17

'I know,' said the surgeon wearily. 'But I can save you the trouble. There's not the slightest chance she'll speak again. The vocal cords are severed.' And even as they spoke, a second doctor came out to say that the girl was dead.

Chapter 4

Behind Proby's head, an old-fashioned blackboard recorded the details of both girls in dusty chalk. In front of him the team of detectives, now doubled to over fifty, listened as he outlined the common factors.

'Tell me if you disagree,' he said, 'but I see three alternatives at this stage. One, it is just possible that these are two disconnected crimes. A shotgun is not an unusual weapon in these parts, and the shot size was different, No. 6 in the first, No. 5 in the second. Second possibility: that there is a link between the two victims which made them both targets of the same murderer. If so, we haven't found it yet. Third, the explanation we can expect the papers to seize on, that there is an indiscriminate lunatic on the loose, with an insatiable urge to murder young women. Even though there is no evidence of a sexual motive.' He paused, watching the rows of young faces, their expressions ranging from Braithwaite's eager frown to Hickock's leaden half-doze.

'There are no joint suspects at this stage. Hippo Doyle was in the Conservative Club at the time of the second murder with half the City Council, and Mary Grogan's boyfriend was at home with his parents. There is no reason to doubt either alibi. All of you have copies of Mrs Doyle's secret correspondence. Any ideas on the mysterious "S"?'

Hickock shrugged. 'Bit of a sexual athlete,' he murmured, 'and likes to talk about it. I'd say he was over thirty, married or has been. Well educated.'

19

'Why?'

'Well, *I* couldn't spell all those words correctly.' Someone sniggered. 'What did the graphologist say?'

'We're still waiting for her report. But I agree. I'd also guess he might be older than Joe here has suggested. Fifty maybe. He makes quite a lot of noise about their sessions, almost as if he feels he's doing better than she might expect.' A couple of the older detectives nodded ruefully.

'Anyway,' said Proby when he wound up the discussion, 'you all know now what you've got to do. But I want to caution you against one preconception.' They looked up inquisitively. 'We've all fallen into the habit of referring to the murderer as 'he'. I don't see anything so far to exclude it being a woman. Be off with you!'

'Tell me again what Doyle said,' he asked Hickock who had stayed behind to check some details on the computer. 'Did he mind being knocked up?'

'Not a bit,' grunted the other. 'Quite the reverse. He said I was to tell you to keep him in touch whenever anything happened, whatever the time of night! I think he means it when he says he'll have a go at the culprit. He's taken his wife's death very hard. I'd say he's lost a stone overnight.'

'Hmmm.' Proby took out a packet of cigarettes and tapped one into his hand. 'I'm not sure I'd blame him.' He stuck the cigarette in his mouth and lit it, breathing in deeply and then blowing the smoke away from Hickock up to the ceiling. It was his first cigarette of the month.

'How are the shotgun checks going?' Julie had come into the room, and was waiting for his attention.

'Fine,' she replied. 'Sixty per cent checked with none out of place. It's a long job in an area like this.'

He shook his head at the breadth of the task. For all the city's dead industrial history, the countryside round Hampton was densely wooded, with little farms in the hills, and larger tracts in the plain beyond. All the farmers kept legal shotguns for use against crows, foxes and other vermin, and quite a few of the city people as well, whether for the clay pigeon clubs or through having a share in one of the sporting syndicates who rented game shooting off the big farming estates. It was a vast endeavour to check them all, and the uniformed branch were already occupied with the approach of Christmas and the Chief Constable's new campaign against drunken driving.

'They know what to look for?'

'Oh yes!' smiled Rootham. 'Trouble is nowadays, the local beat copper doesn't know his patch as you and I once did.'

'Hark at the old man!' shouted Hickock with glee. 'Why, when I was on the beat, you were in your effing pram.'

'Get to work, you two,' snapped Proby, suddenly impatient. 'I want this one rounded up before another girl gets slaughtered.'

Julie looked at him sympathetically after the others had hurried off, wrapping their coats around them against the windy chill outside.

'You think it's a serial killer,' she said, and not as a question.

He nodded, drawing on his cigarette. 'I reckon. And I don't know a damned thing about him. Or her.' He blew her a kiss, and picking his hat off the desk, he hurried off to brief the Chief Constable.

Identifying a murderer is usually the least of a policeman's task. Eighty-three per cent of murder victims know their killer, and in most of those cases it is a member of their immediate family. Proving it in court may not be so easy. Of the remaining cases, most are in pursuit of a crime, so that there may be other sources of help, informers mainly, or matching previous convictions. If only he could identify a common link, a common motive, there might be some hope of progress. But if this *was* his worst fear, a totally random homicidal maniac, then his only hope was that the killer would make a mistake, and be caught.

'How's it all coming along, Jim?' The Chief Constable

was an ambitious man. He had been at Hampton for ten years and further promotion, even a knighthood, was not out of reach. He took trouble to cultivate the local magnates, was on Christian name terms with the Lord Lieutenant, and was highly thought of at Bramshill for his lectures on 'The Modern Policeman in Society'.

Proby, watching his smooth hard face framed by slicked-back silvered hair, fought back a sarcastic answer. He shook his head.

'Nothing positive. I'm very grateful for the extra men.' The Chief waved an expansive hand.

'There's more if you need them. I've spoken to the Chairman of the Police Committee. They've given me carte blanche, within reason. It's an ugly case. I want it cleared up quickly.'

'You got my report?'

The Chief looked vaguely around, but Proby knew this vagueness was a deliberate pose, a sort of pseudo-gentility that the Chief, in his adopted social circle, believed to be smart. Underneath he was quick, efficient and merciless. He knew every word of Proby's report and his fainéant approach signified approval.

'You've checked the licence holders?'

'Three quarters of the way through.'

'With all those men?'

'I'm using twelve to stake out the murder scenes.'

'Is that really necessary?'

'It's the best chance I've got, the way I see it.'

'You're certain it's a serial?'

'Oh yes. Twenty to one on, maybe higher. Those two girls had nothing in common. Five years apart, different schools and different upbringing. One slept around, the other was a virgin.'

'Extraordinary what facts we learn about the victims,' mused the Chief. 'We often know more about them than the criminals.'

'Quite.'

'Anything I can do to help, James?' The Chief prided

himself on knowing his men on friendly terms. To this end he kept a sheaf of photographs with the relevant names in the top drawer of his desk. He liked to think it showed he was close to the roots.

'Yes,' replied Proby unexpectedly. 'There is.'

The Chief's eyebrows rose slightly. 'In that?'

'Your drink-driving campaign.'

'. . . yes?' This was very dear to the Chief's heart, since it had been publicly commented on in the *Daily Telegraph*. It was all part of raising his profile.

'Could you intensify it?'

'*Intensify* it?' This was a first. A suspicious glance darted at Proby from under the supercilious arch of the Chief's manicured eyebrows. Was this man presuming to pull his leg?

'Yes,' Proby leant forward. 'The odds are on the murderer moving by car or van. He or she couldn't walk far with a gun, even one that folds under a coat. And this is no poacher's .410. It's a twelve bore, and from the pattern, Ballistics reckon it has thirty-inch barrels. Now there's no need to alarm people unnecessarily. But this way you can be stopping cars at random – particularly cars with single drivers – and they'll just put it down to your drink-drive policy.'

The Chief frowned. It was a good idea. And if anything came of it, he could count on wide publicity. He nodded swiftly. 'I'll spread the word,' he said. 'I like it.'

'I thought you might,' said Proby, but he said it to himself.

Chapter 5

The first people to get picked up by the stake-outs were a couple living on a houseboat. Twice they drifted past the towpath, the engine idling, and the man photographing the very spot where the body had been found, even though no trace of a police presence betrayed its sad history. The first time Allan spotted them, his mind was concentrating too hard on his girlfriend to think twice about them until after they had drifted out of sight beyond the lock-keeper's cottage. But the longer he sat there, the more an insistent question about the photographer kept intruding itself at the back of his mind. He had just tagged its significance and was reaching for his radio when there they were again. The woman was complaining about something, but the man was single-mindedly snapping the empty towpath, his camera remaining fixed on that single spot which should have been no different to him than all the rest of the scenery.

'Hi! You there. On the *D'Artagnan*!'

Allan's shout gave the man such a fright that he nearly overbalanced.

'What do you want?' he shouted back angrily. 'You shouldn't cry out like that. Might cause a nasty accident.'

'Pull over,' said Allan in his normal voice. After all, they were now only a few feet apart.

'Why should we?' Now the woman was joining in. 'What's it to you what we do?'

Allan flashed his badge. 'Police,' he said. 'Come on. Make it snappy.' Hickock, who had been taking a nap behind the tin shed, was rubbing his eyes.

'Now what?' he said. Allan walked over and told him. Grudgingly the man was tying his boat up to a tree across the towpath.

'We're not supposed to do this,' he grumbled. 'What if someone comes along on a bicycle?'

'If they can't see that rope,' replied Allan, 'they shouldn't be on a bicycle.'

'Where are you taking us?'

'Just up to the station,' said Hickock from beside her. The man was now seated in the front of the car beside Allan. They had called in and Proby was returning from the docks to interview the couple.

'I'll take the woman first,' he decided. 'Keep the other one in the waiting room. Give him some coffee or something. And,' as an afterthought, 'get him to write a couple of sentences. You'll think of something.'

'I'm not sure you ought to be doing this,' the woman said when she was brought in, a dumpy over-made-up creature with a London accent. 'I don't think you've got the right.'

'I'm sure you wouldn't want to obstruct the police now, would you?' inquired Proby genially. 'Why would you want to do that?' Her expression changed and she forced a smile.

'Oh no,' she said. 'But we weren't doing anything wrong. I suppose it's about that old poll tax thingee?' He shook his head.

'Let us start with the basics.' He smiled at her. 'Your name?'

'Elizabeth Sylvester.'

'Married?'

'No.' Her eyes dared him to show disapproval.

'Divorced?'

'No.' She must be about the same age as him.

'Date of birth?'

'The twelfth of July 1938.' They were twins! He wrote it down without comment.

'You live on the boat?'

'Yes.'

'How long?'

'Eight years.' Her answers were delivered in a flat bored monotone, her lips compressed in a thin line, as if she had decided to put up with whatever he threw at her.

'Your friend's name?'

'Sam White.' He nodded.

'You draw Social Security?'

She smiled. 'You've got quite a knack of asking offensive questions in your nice quiet way,' she said, with an appraising glance. 'But, yes. We draw Social Security from the Canal Street branch. As a couple,' she emphasized. 'There's no jiggery-pokery about it. Sam's got a disability allowance too.'

'What's wrong with him?'

'Did his back in, working for the Post Office.'

'I see.' Proby leant back in his chair and paused. Above the door, the electric clock reminded him he had not yet had lunch.

'Tell me about Sam.'

She shrugged. 'What do you want to know?'

'Is he keen on photography?'

'Not much.'

'Do you travel that stretch of the canal regularly?'

She leant forward, her frayed pullover revealing a scraggy neck. 'Let me tell you,' she said. 'We've never been on that stretch before, and after today, I doubt we'll be on it again! What've you got down there – atomic bombs?'

'Does he have other women?'

She pushed the table back abruptly and stood up. 'I'm not putting up with this,' she said. 'I want a solicitor. We've got rights like everyone else!'

Proby sighed. 'Take her outside,' he said to the patient Rootham. 'And let's have her friend in.'

'What's she been saying?'

The man from the barge had a hoarse truculent voice that grated on Proby's nerves. He had a headache coming on, perhaps even the first signs of flu. 'I'll have a cup of coffee,' he said to Allan who had put his head round the door. 'Ask Julie to make it, will you?'

'She'd say anything that comes into her head.' The man looked like a drinker, with blue-veined cheeks and a bulbous nose. Rootham slid a piece of paper in front of Proby. On it the man had written, 'My name is Samuel White. I was born on 8 October 1935 and I am divorced.' The writing was totally dissimilar to that in the late Mrs Doyle's love letters. This was no surprise. It was impossible to imagine Mr White as a young girl's delight.

'So.' Proby rubbed his forehead. 'What was so interesting that you wanted to photograph it twice?' Why not put his cards on the table? He was no longer interested. He simply didn't believe in this man as a murderer.

'How do you mean like?'

'You were using your camera?' Rootham took over, sensing Proby's lack of concentration.

'Yeh.'

'You photographed the footpath?'

'Well – you've took the film. You ought to know.'

'It's still being developed. Suppose you tell me?'

The man shrugged. 'It's a pretty spot.'

'But you came back?'

'Yeh. Well – we were just having a jaunt.'

'So tell us. What was so special about that spot?'

The man looked at his hands. 'Are you going to charge me?' he asked sullenly.

'Worrying about the poll tax?' asked Proby softly.

The man turned angry eyes at him. 'What's that to you?' he asked. 'And what services do we get, I'd like to know?'

'The police?' suggested Rootham, smiling.

'Oh *thanks*!' the man said with heavy sarcasm.

'The photographs?' prodded Proby. 'That's all we want to know – we've got nothing to do with the Council, unless you give us bother.'

The man shrugged. 'That's where Hippo Doyle's missus

got blown away. Everybody knows that. Some of the lads up at the Wiggly Worm wanted a snap. Hippo's none too popular at the Wiggly Worm.'

'And how did you know the exact spot?'

The man drew a folded map out of his pocket. 'Willie marked it for me,' he said. 'Willie the lock-keeper. It's his brother as keeps the Wiggly Worm.'

Proby, whose head was beginning to throb with painful persistency, just wanted him to go away.

'You'd better get some lunch,' said Julie when she brought in his coffee. 'You look *awful*.' He managed a grin.

When he got home, he found the house locked up and the fridge empty except for the previous day's congealed soup. There was no note on the mat. Sheila had long since given up expecting him by day.

Chapter 6

Just north of the city, the river wound through a steep valley, its banks thickly wooded with pine trees. Here and there, the larches had shed their needles, giving occasional relief from the dense covering that shrouded the little path that led down towards a deserted boathouse beside the sluggish water. A heavy frost glittered on the trees and on the exposed patches of ground; otherwise, all was shadowed and silent. Behind an immense fir, the figure in the white mackintosh waited patiently. Now and then, an anxious face was raised at some distant sound, perhaps a pigeon settling in a tree or a rabbit scampering across the hard ground. A thin silvery wisp of smoke betrayed the presence of a soothing cigarette. At last came the awaited sound – the sound of a woman's voice, singing in the cold clear air. The cigarette fell and was ground into the crisp mixture of pine needles and decayed bracken. Along the path, a young woman, her pale hair tied back in a green and gold scarf, was walking briskly, singing out loud and swinging her carrier bag to the rhythm. She had the sort of beauty that startled – that conjunction of perfect features lit by high spirits, today accentuated by the clear frosty air, so that her cheeks shone with natural colour. At the sound of a metallic click, she stopped, looking round, but without alarm.

'Hello!' she said, smiling as the figure moved out of the shadows. 'Why are you looking like that?'

The sound of the shots echoed sharply in the icy stillness – the first two almost together, and then a third, and a fourth. Wiping away some tears, the murderer carefully collected the ejected cartridge casings, picked up the cigarette stub and, shouldering the gun, turned sharply into the trees and pursued an apparently familiar course through the trackless woodland.

In Hampton, the streets were full of Christmas shoppers. The High Street traders had combined to erect elaborate decorations strung across the road, depicting Santa Claus and his reindeer, illuminated at night by hundreds of coloured bulbs set in spangled silver paper. Sheila Proby, weighed down by two bags full of presents, turned into the little patisserie with a sigh of relief. Her ankles were aching, and her mind was full of the delights of a chocolate eclair. She sank down into the familiar velvet couchette with a smile of anticipation.

'The usual?' The little waitress had frizzy red hair, a doughy skin and grey eyes that sparkled with complicity.

'Yes please, Wendy.' Sheila sat back, luxuriating in the warmth of the room and the support her back received from the generously padded seat.

'There you are.' A richly confected eclair, bursting with thick cream, confronted her, and was shortly joined by a brimming mug of cocoa.

'This is heaven,' she sighed to herself, sniffing the aroma.

'Hello there!' Sheila looked up to see Mollie Rootham making her way briskly between the tables. 'No fear!' said Mollie, waving away the menu. 'Just a cup of tea for me. As it comes.' She sat down, covertly noting Sheila's ample curves and wondering, not for the first time, how such a pretty woman could indulge herself so shamelessly in extra calories.

'What have you got there?' Between mouthfuls, Sheila pulled out her presents, a mobile telephone for her father, a blue and white Wedgwood ornament for her mother, some plastic toys for her baby nieces and, heaviest of all, a magnum of champagne for her sister and brother-in-law.

'Very nice,' said Mollie, eyeing the vintage. 'And what about Jim?'

Sheila shrugged. 'Oh I haven't thought yet,' she said. 'He never notices what I give him anyway. If he's there.'

Mollie sipped her tea. She, too, was married to a policeman, and had always known and accepted the interferences that went with such a job. She was very conscious of the value of cultivating her husband's seniors, and certainly wasn't going to jeopardize his career by criticizing Sheila.

'One more?' The waitress had returned with the plate of eclairs.

'Why not?' said Sheila, raising her plate. 'Have one on me,' she added, noting Mollie's disapproving eye.

'No fear!'

'Worried about your figure?' Mollie, a size 8, was still as slender as a teenager. She nodded.

'Well, I'm not,' Sheila laughed, 'and if Jim minds, he can stuff it!' There was an awkward pause. 'So what are you up to?'

Mollie shrugged. 'Just window-shopping,' she said. 'I'm collecting the twins in ten minutes. They're at ballet class.'

Sheila looked at her watch. Having no children herself, the subject was one she tried to ignore, or, better, avoid. It wasn't a nagging little sore, it was a deep and poisoned wound, which sometimes made her want to climb on to a table and shout, 'Look at me! I have never conceived. I am not a real woman. I am EMPTY!' In the past Jim had tried to console her, to emphasize that it was no one's fault, least of all hers. But she had managed to silence him at last, punishing him for her pain. And she punished herself through eating, trying to stifle the inner voice and spoil her looks with sheer weight of food. Perversely, no man had ever complained about her swelling, barren flesh. She spooned in the last mouthful of crisp pastry thickly smeared with rich dark chocolate. Another way to punish herself was through sex. Sucking down the last wisp of cream, she licked her lips. If only she could be sufficiently degraded, might that not dull the pain?

Leaving a generous tip for Wendy, she gathered up her parcels and left Mollie to finish her tea by herself. Outside the sky was darker now, and the distant thump of the Salvation Army band, up by the Town Hall, gave her a comfortable seasonal feeling.

'Hello, gorgeous!'

Without thinking, she had collided with a man coming out of the arcade. Men, to Sheila, presented a perpetual challenge. It was not really that she deliberately sought sexual adventure, but something deep within her stirred at contact with, sometimes just the sight of, a man. She looked up, prepared to snub him, only to recognize Henry Bryant, their church-warden.

'Hello,' she replied with a cautious smile. He was an attractive man, slightly older than her husband. He did something indeterminate at the local army barracks, and figured all too often in her regular private fantasies. His dark brown eyes had long lashes and were disconcertingly spaced far apart, making her feel as if she were squinting when she gazed up at them, noting the intriguing curl of his thick dark brows.

'Christmas shopping?' she asked in what she hoped was a light-hearted voice.

'What else? Let me take that for you.' He slipped his arm under hers and carried off the heavy bags with practised ease.

'You don't know where I'm going,' she protested.

'Whither thou goest . . .' He had a charming smile and always showed a flattering interest in her figure. 'Can I buy you a drink?'

'That would be nice.' They turned into the Paradise Arms and settled down at a table by the fire.

'Gin and tonic?'

'Yes, please.' She watched him ordering with the calm certainty of a man who was used to getting his own way.

'To you!' he said. 'And to your beautiful green eyes!' She gulped down the refreshing liquid, conscious of his lips. They were full, and luscious, curving up into deep folds that, running down from either side of his nose, gave his face a slightly comical look.

'We should do this more often,' he said, and lowered his glance to the swell of her dress.

Is this how it starts, she wondered, was it like this before? Is it so obvious that I am looking for adventure? She met his glance and held it provocatively, feeling that familiar frisson that her husband no longer evoked.

'How's Anne?' she asked involuntarily, but he only laughed.

' "Had I but world enough and time . . ." ' and brushed her hand with his.

She stared.

'It's a poem,' he said. 'It's about unnecessary delays in a busy busy world.'

'I don't know it,' she said, hearing her own voice as if from a long way off, 'tell me more.'

'Later,' he replied.

'Where?' She could hardly breathe.

He looked at her, his face suddenly hardening.

'Now?'

'Why not?' Perhaps the gin had gone to her head. She wanted to touch him. He passed her a key with as little ceremony as if it had been a cigarette.

'Fourteen, Timpson Street. Do you know where that is?' She nodded, unable to speak.

'Five minutes then.' He stood up. 'Let me take the parcels.' Carrying them in front of him, he walked over to the bar, paid the bill and left her awash with the surge of her emotions.

An hour later as she cradled his sweating body on the floor of the empty house, wriggling luxuriously in the thick pile of the rug, she wondered how many other women he must have enjoyed here, making them respond as shamelessly as she had, gorging themselves to the full. It was too soon to start worrying about going home, about masking her new excitement and more particularly about hiding the livid bruises where he had bitten her breasts. Just for the moment she was content to lie there, experiencing an unfamiliar sense of physical and mental peace, almost of floating in a dream world, while at the same time reassuringly weighed down by Henry's bulk. Henry Bryant. Hers! Somewhere in the city she heard the sound of a siren.

Chapter 7

At the ambulance control HQ, a small Nissen hut at the back of St Hugh's, the mental handicap unit of the Hampton District General Hospital, the two control officers were enjoying a quiet, if illicit, smoke. The red light set in the ceiling flickered on, and the younger of the two, a slight man with a sallow foxy face, snatched up the telephone in front of him. As he did so, the other, with a sigh, stubbed out his cigarette and picked a blank form off the pile at his elbow.

'All right, love. I'll repeat that. Emergency. Junction of the B6079 and the C514. That's in the woods north of Claxby St Anne. Police in attendance. We'll get on with it. I'm timing this call at 14.07.' He put down the receiver, took the form from his colleague and deftly inserted it into the time clock which snapped at it like a hungry crocodile, punching the digits indelibly through the paper. The exact time was thus registered both on the form and on the automatic machine under his desk that had begun, as soon as the red light had illuminated, to record his telephone conversation. He now had 120 seconds to despatch an ambulance in order to meet his employing authority's obligations.

'Who've we got?'

'Where is it?'

'North – must be seven miles at least.'

'Christ!' They peered at the large scale map on the opposite wall.

'Two-oh-seven is coming back from Castlewick.'

'Yeah – but it's got two children from Mental Handicap, hasn't it?'

'Well – they could budge up.'

'Leave it out – this sounds like a messy one.'

'Two-nineteen is free at the DGH.'

'They haven't had their dinner yet.' They looked anxiously at the clock: forty seconds to go.

'Where's 203?'

'Don't ask me – he's still wandering round Larch Meadow with that tarty Rehabilitation case. Anyway, this needs two men.'

'Two-nineteen it is then.' He reached for the microphone and switched it on, automatically re-activating the recorder.

'Control to 219. Come in please.' The crackle of static filled their musty office as the loudspeakers responded. 'Control calling 219 – come on, George, for God's sake!'

'Two-nineteen! What do you want?'

'Emergency case – Claxby St Anne – we'll give you detailed instructions once you're off the ring road.'

'We're just off to the canteen!'

'Sorry, mate.' The officer wondered if the other had forgotten about the recorder.

'What time have you?' At that moment the time clock gave a wary click.

'Fourteen-ten.' He sighed; another case he'd have to explain to the Deputy Chief.

'Fourteen-ten and I'm hungry.'

'On your way.' The red light started to flicker again. It looked like being a busy afternoon.

It was nearly six by the time the young woman's body had been cleared for removal by Proby and delivered by the ambulance crew to the mortuary, wrapped in a double thickness of impermeable plastic. The two-man crew, accompanied by young Braithwaite, waited by the lift doors in silence. At last the lift bell rang and the doors slid open. They exchanged gloomy looks and wheeled the

36

trolley in, pressing the button marked Basement. The lift descended with maddening slowness, and they wheeled their burden, almost at a trot, down the subterranean passage, past hissing pipes and rows of dusty cables, to a point where the linoleum, hitherto gleamingly clean, deteriorated to the point of disintegration. The cause of this damage was immediately apparent. A long incline stretched upwards before them, and down this, vibrating noisily, came a small green and gold machine, highly polished and carelessly steered by a tall old man in white overalls. As he reached the foot of the slope, he swung the machine's wheel deftly to the right, so that it slewed round, with a squeal of protesting rubber, and came to a stop next to the trolley with its frail cargo.

'Strewth!' He blew his nose loudly between his fingers. 'What have you got there?'

'Another of these poor girls.'

'Shotgun job?'

George, the fatter of the two ambulance men, nodded. 'A real looker.'

'Clip it on then.' Thankfully the ambulance men slipped the hook of the trolley over the rail of his vehicle, and watched the little procession, with Braithwaite still in mute attendance, rolling away up the slope. Up it went, round a corner and out of their sight where it nosed its way through a thick plastic curtain and into the autopsy precincts. There Weatherill, the principal mortician, was swapping jokes with the coroner and the histopathologist, already scrubbed up and waiting. A telephone buzzed somewhere among the bottles.

'Yes?' The mortician had the face if not the manner of a circus clown, with bright red cheeks and gloriously black bushy brows. 'Right-o!' He turned to the others. 'Dr Milligan will be here in three minutes. Is it tagged?' While Braithwaite watched, more worried about his own reaction in an unfamiliar environment than about the corpse, an assistant hurried round to tie a blue label on an outstretched toe.

'Nice shade of varnish,' he remarked. The coroner, a short man with a pink-striped shirt, retched discreetly into his handkerchief. Milligan came through an outer door, already changed and masked, and together the professionals formed a group round their victim, like so many vultures, and edged the trolley up against the shallow white mould that was to receive the remains. They heaved her into this receptacle and pulled away the sheeting. A massive updraught from the fans above, designed to sweep away all scent of mortality, filled the room with its violent noise.

'Have you got all your Christmas presents?' Braithwaite turned to find the little coroner, his face distorted with some strong emotion, fear perhaps, or just nausea, looking up at him beseechingly. He shrugged. It felt better to be beside someone who could cope even less than himself.

Dr Milligan had removed his mask, and was grappling with something heavy.

'You see?' they heard him say to the nodding red face of the mortician. Together they worked away, amid the stink of formaldehyde, as this organ and that was removed, examined and plunged into jars for further detailed study.

By the time Proby arrived, the coroner had long since disappeared. 'The same?'

Dr Milligan nodded his head angrily. 'What a bastard!'

'Anything new?'

The doctor shook his head. As he pulled off his gloves and followed the other medical staff through the opaque pitted curtain that led to the showers, their conversation had already turned to the need to provide extra storage space in the refrigerated storage room.

'Is it true they've found another body in the woods?'

DC Hickock looked up from his drink that evening to see a stooped cadaverous man pulling up a stool beside him. George Pratt was the crime reporter for the

Hampton Gazette, whose usual thin diet of car theft and missing video-recorders was enlivened every Friday and Saturday night by staking out the Casualty Ward of Hampton District General Hospital. With rising unemployment and continental licensing hours, the potential for promotion from page 5 (City News) to a banner front page headline (with consequential bonus) was well worth the effort. But an hour ago his editor had told him to drop everything except the recent murders.

Hickock nodded. 'That's what I heard. I'll have a pint, thank you, George.'

'Any details yet?' The reporter slid a couple of coins across to the barman.

Hickock shook his head. 'I've been given the evening off,' he said. 'I'm just off home for a kip. But I will give you a call if I learn anything worthwhile.'

'Staking out the canal?' inquired the reporter shrewdly.

Hickock shrugged. 'The Docks. But keep it under your hat. We won't catch anybody if they know we're waiting for them.'

'Do you really think a smart man like this is going to be that silly?' The reporter was drinking soda water.

'If he's mad enough to do in young girls, he might be mad enough for anything,' muttered Hickock.

'The Hampton Ripper?'

'Or Blaster. Or whatever. He's got to be off his rocker. Those were good-looking kids. You could understand a rapist. But just blowing them away. Must be a nutter.'

'What does Proby think?'

'He reckons it's a woman.'

'A woman! How does he make that out? Here, have another.'

'Thanks.' Hickock's eyes were just a little unfocused, damp red blotches appearing across his cheeks like rosy fingers. 'Don't say I told you. But that's his line.'

'What about Hippo then?'

'Well, he's got to be the chief suspect, hasn't he, whatever the Mayor says.'

'What's the Mayor got to do with it?'

'They were supposed to be swilling champagne together the whole evening!'

'Can you get me copies of those dirty letters?'

Hickock wiped his eyes angrily. 'I've told you no before. That's too far.'

'It's worth a hundred.'

'You serious? A hundred *pounds*?'

'Keep your voice down,' muttered the reporter. 'I've got five twenties in my pocket when you hand over two of those copies. My editor would like to see them.'

'Proby'd do me if he found out.'

'He'd never put it down to you, and a hundred pounds would buy a lot of Christmas presents.'

'I'll see what I can do.' Hickock emptied his glass and the reporter watched a thin drizzle of beer running down his companion's collar.

'You do that,' he said and, picking up his overcoat, he turned his inquisitive nose towards the mortuary.

When Proby got back that evening, it was to find his house ablaze with lights, and unaccustomed preparations being made for an elaborate dinner. Sheila came hurrying out of the kitchen with a bright solicitous smile.

'Are you very tired, darling?'

He nodded, luxuriating in the warmth of her embrace. 'A bit.'

'Come and sit down while I make a pot of tea.' He followed her gratefully into the kitchen.

'Steak and kidney,' she said, unnecessarily, because the room was full of the aromatic scent of the stew. His spirits rose, but nevertheless he knew he had bad news to break.

'There's been a very bad development,' he said heavily, as she busied herself at the cooker. 'Anne Bryant's been murdered.' Whatever reaction he may have expected, the crash of the casserole on the stone floor behind him was so shockingly loud that he jumped. Sheila, her white face staring open-mouthed, ignored the spreading mess.

'Anne? Dead?'

'Yes. They found her this morning in the woods. Same as before.'

'Shot?' she whispered, placing one quivering hand on her cheek.

'Let me.' He had bent down and was rather helplessly spooning the stew back into the metal pot. She turned and walked out of the room.

Locking herself in the bathroom, she leant heavily back against the door, resting her pounding head against the cool silk of her wrap, and stared at her reflection in the mirror. Her mind was confused by a ravaging blur of competing fears. Anne dead? Henry a suspect? Henry in danger? She his alibi? *She his alibi!* But surely Anne had been killed in the morning.

'Sheila! Darling? Are you all right?' In normal circumstances, the sound of her husband's loving anxious voice would have soothed her; now its only effect was to frighten and disturb her further.

'Go away!' she heard herself shouting. 'Leave me alone!'

A long silence followed. Then she heard his heavy footsteps retreating down the stairs of their home.

Chapter 8

Henry Bryant was sitting smoking at his desk when he heard Proby's car on the gravel outside. The house had once been the rectory when the suburb of Hampton where they both lived had been a separate village. But post-war sprawl had submerged both Graceby and its neighbouring stone villages of Limpsey and Stockard St Peter under a wave of red brick, so that the old stone houses with their heavy slate roofs stood out almost like interlopers among the ranks of rusty villas. St Jude's Church, Graceby, tall and slender, with its extravagant Elizabethan clerestory and delicate crocketed spire, was the sole proof that life had flourished here since the Middle Ages. Three hundred years of architectural silence followed, punctuated by the early Victorian rectory and half a dozen surviving village houses built in the local stone. All the rest had gone: the Elizabethan thatches, the Georgian terraced cottages, the High Victorian gothic school. All the more reason for Henry to celebrate his stewardship of the Old Rectory, which he and Anne had lovingly re-created with a riot of Pugin wall-papers and heavy fringed hangings that draped every window and doorway. Somewhere deep within the house, a bell jangled. Henry put down his cigar and went out into the dark hallway. He could see the familiar bulk of his friend and fellow churchgoer standing in the porch. Jim Proby's face was in the shadows, but a wintry sunbeam shining through the porch's stained glass window cast a livid red stain across his shirt, giving him almost the appearance of one of the victims.

'My dear fellow!' Henry hurried through the inner doorway and took the proffered hand.

'I'm dreadfully sorry,' said Jim heavily. 'We both are.'

It was the following morning. Sheila had taken herself off to the spare room and spent the night there, leaving him to stare at the ceiling, reflecting morosely on the unpredictability of married life. Rising early, as was his habit, he had not liked to disturb her. They had both liked, and greatly admired, Anne Bryant, not only for her beauty, but also for her discreet and unselfconsciously performed good works within the three amalgamated parishes. If Henry was just a little too much 'the squire', Anne veered quite the other way, enthusiastically but self-effacingly promoting a sense of community life in what might, without her, have simply evolved into yet another dormitory suburb of Hampton. Instead, they still had a Sunday school, an infants' playgroup, an amateur dramatics season and a thriving branch of the Women's Institute. To have achieved all this, and still not be hated, Sheila had observed, was the mark of a very clever woman. And now, hardly thirty, she was dead.

'You're very kind,' murmured Henry, taking the other's coat.

'It must have been a terrible shock,' said Jim, taking in Henry's black tie. It hardly seemed the moment to ask if he always kept one by him, just in case. Knowing Henry, he probably did.

'Coffee?'

'Please!'

'Black, two sugars, isn't it?'

Jim nodded gratefully, settling himself into the familiar deep red leather armchair beside the fire. It was a low room, with arched gothic windows giving out over a lawn to the stone wall that bounded the graveyard. Beyond reared the great west window of the church. On the desk he could see a heap of unopened Christmas cards along with other post. Besides being vicar's warden, Henry worked at the Ministry of Defence establishment out at Castlewick, and ran one of the shooting syndicates on the

Claxby Hall estate. It was in one of the woods under his care that Anne had been found by the estate forester.

'How's that?' Henry had returned and gently set down a steaming mug.

'Just what I needed!' It was indeed his first sustenance of the day. He hadn't liked to make a noise in the kitchen for fear of waking Sheila.

'I imagine this isn't entirely a social call.' If Henry's tone was dry, it was perhaps unintentional. Jim looked at him, and nodded.

'We have to stop these killings,' he said, 'and, yes, I need your help, even at a time like this.'

'You know I'll do anything!'

'Of course. I need to ask you a few questions. And I should like to have a thorough look through Anne's things.'

'Is that really necessary?'

'Yes.' Silence fell. The two men's eyes met. 'I'm sure you understand.'

'Fire away then.'

'Did Anne often walk in the Claxby woods?'

Henry paused for thought. 'From time to time. She liked the solitude. Perhaps twice a week in the summer, less in the colder weather.'

'Who knew she would be there yesterday?'

'You don't think she met this maniac by chance then?'

'She may well have done,' replied Jim equably, 'but I should like to eliminate the other possibilities.'

'Well, of course, I knew. And Mrs Bertram – our daily woman, you know.'

Jim had taken out a small green notebook, and was taking down various points. 'Anyone else?'

'No, not that I know of. Perhaps the vicar. Mrs Bertram would know. She's in the kitchen now.'

'I can talk to her later. Who might Anne expect to meet in the woods?'

'What the devil do you mean?'

Henry's outburst took Jim entirely by surprise. He

raised his hands, 'Nothing offensive, I promise you, but perhaps a gamekeeper, or Luke the man who found her, or one of your shooting friends?'

Henry looked almost ashamed by his sudden truculence. 'I'm sorry,' he said. 'Of course, I see now. Yes, Clark the keeper, or his son Nat certainly. The forester, as you say. Maybe old Colonel Bridgeman – he owns the land, as you know. Or Brewster, the agent. Not that I'd expect to see any of them. Most days when I go, it's as quiet as the grave.'

'And did you go yesterday?' A quiet question, quietly put. Again their eyes met.

'No.'

'I know you'll understand that I have to ask for your movements yesterday.'

This time Henry smiled. 'This can't be easy for you, old chap,' he said.

Jim shrugged. 'I thought you'd rather deal with me.' He sipped his coffee. It was delicious.

'Definitely.' Henry picked up his cigar and re-lit it with a long match, thoughtfully blowing out the blue aromatic smoke. 'Would you like one of these?' Jim shook his head.

'I've almost given up,' he said. 'Sheila never has liked the smell.'

'Ah, but these Havanas smell wonderful! As to yesterday,' he took another puff, 'I had the day off work. So I went out early to have a look round Hills and Makin's for a present for Anne. Really I spent the whole day in the town centre.'

'See any friends?'

'Yes! I ran into Sheila in the High Street, and we had a quick drink in the Paradise Arms.' Jim wrote down his wife's name without comment.

'What sort of time was that?'

'Oh? One o'clockish.'

'No one else?'

'Not that I noticed. I got back here to find your Sergeant . . . Rowston? . . . waiting on the doorstep. The

45

funny thing was, I sort of knew as soon as I saw him.'

'Rootham. Knew what?'

'Well, that something dreadful had happened to Anne. This maniac has made us all cowards.'

'Did Anne have any enemies that you know of?' The change of tack caused Henry to apply another match to the cigar.

'No, definitely not. You knew her as well as anyone. Can you imagine her having an enemy?'

Jim shook his head. It wasn't a very likely surmise. 'Forgive me,' he said softly, 'but . . .'

'But what?' snapped the other. 'Did we get on? Did she have lovers? Is that what you're ever so gently approaching?'

'Exactly.' Twenty years of similar interviews had hardened the policeman's reflexes. This was his job – to trample on the sorest corns of grieving relatives, but in the cause of justice. If you believed in the cause, then the job had to be done. Henry glowered at him.

'We had the occasional row. What couple doesn't? Over silly things. Her mother. My sister. The drawing-room curtains. You must know what I mean. But no! We were very happy, and I hardly think she'd have had time for a lover.'

'Thank you.' Jim stood up, suddenly towering over his friend. 'I'll have a quiet snoop round. Would you mind opening your post, and Anne's, and telling me if there's anything interesting?'

Henry shrugged. 'Make yourself at home,' he said. 'As I say, Mrs Bertram's in the kitchen. You know your way.'

Mrs Bertram, a stout old lady with blue-rinsed curls, was not alone in the high-ceilinged kitchen, with its rows of copper pans and moulds displayed across the confident red walls. Detective Sergeant Rootham, his face contorted with frustrated impatience, was sitting at the scrubbed central table staring angrily at his companion. The room smelt strongly of something disagreeable.

'There you are, Mr Proby!' she cried triumphantly. 'I was just telling your friend, there's nobody like Mrs Proby when it comes to liking a piece of my jam sponge.'

'I've been trying to explain,' said the sorely tried Rootham, 'that we need to know about Mrs Bryant's movements.'

'Poor soul!' said her former housekeeper, unable to keep a distinct nuance of guilty pleasure out of her voice. 'I was only telling our Enid, you remember her, Mr Proby, my brother Arthur's second girl, well! . . .'

'Mrs Bertram!' Even the normally imperturbable Proby could not suppress a note of irritation. Really, she absolutely stank! 'We do need your co-operation. I'm sure you want to help me to catch whoever did this.'

'Oh yes,' she said, impervious to all but the muddled jumble of her own thoughts, 'I'm sure you'll catch him. Why, only the other day, she was standing just where you are now, and do you know what she said . . .?'

'I'm going upstairs,' cut in Proby. 'Sergeant Rootham will take your statement.' He was rewarded by a glance of despairing reproach from the latter.

The old house had two staircases. A heavily carved front staircase of varnished oak made its way, vertically punctuated by a series of severely scowling eagles perched on the newel posts at each turn, up from the hallway to a curtained archway on the first floor. But in the kitchen corridor, a gloomy space decorated only with some faded school group photographs and a print of a herd of cattle struggling through a wintry landscape, a second stair, steep and straight, led through a sprung door with shaded glass panels to a group of small bedrooms overlooking Lime Meadow, the once new but now distressed council estate used for problem families from central Hampton. Though carefully decorated with tiny-flowered paper and bright chintz material, it was obvious these rooms were hardly if ever used. There was a dank, slightly fetid smell about them. Running his finger along the top of a sash, Proby was not surprised to find it black with dust. The mummified corpse of a long-dead spider squatted beside the waste-paper basket. The Bryants had had no children – perhaps these rooms had been waiting hopefully?

Five steps at the end of the little corridor outside led up to the main part of the upstairs floor, where he found what was obviously Henry and Anne's room, a big square chamber with a high four-poster bed, hung with yellow silk, with a tiled bathroom leading off on one side, and on the other a small pink sitting room with a satinwood desk in the window overlooking the graveyard. He could hear Henry moving about immediately below. Without feeling remotely guilty, since it was after all his job, Proby rummaged quietly through all the drawers. Then he crossed the corridor, where two more doors led into a guest suite of two bedrooms, a small dressing room and an even smaller bathroom. These rooms looked over the drive, and were distinctly cold. Clearly they had not been expecting guests for Christmas. He walked back into Anne's little sitting room.

A heap of Christmas presents, all carefully wrapped in scarlet tissue paper with broad silver ribbon, sat on the floor beside her desk, while on it a gold pen lay across half a dozen tiny seasonal labels. He lifted the pen. 'To my darling Henry, with all my love.' 'Henry, dearest, always yours.' 'Henry, I love you.' With a sigh, Proby turned away. Then, being a methodical man, he turned back, sat down and, using a small razor blade, he very carefully undid each present in turn: a bottle of eau de cologne, a gold fountain pen with the initials H.L.B., two silk shirts from a London haberdasher, a book of modern poetry, an enamel regimental brooch and a miniature leather travelling clock with the same initials as the pen. Again he sighed, and hearing more movement below, he very carefully wrapped them all up again, securing them with the roll of double-sided tape he had found in the centre drawer. If previous years were anything to go by, that was the nearest he'd get to opening Christmas presents of any sort! Then he went back downstairs.

'Any luck?' Henry Bryant had obviously decided to make the best of his predicament, and greeted his equivocal guest with almost a smile.

Proby shrugged. 'I never know what I'm looking for,' he said, refusing the silent offer of a drink from the tray behind Henry's chair. 'But it's as well to cover every angle.' The room was thick with smoke.

'Could you get any sense out of Mrs Bertram?'

'Not much.' They both smiled now. 'Poor Rootham's out there still trying. I expect we'll need to talk later today or tomorrow.'

'If there's anything I can do...?' Henry's voice died away.

'I know.' They shook hands. 'And as I say, Sheila feels as deeply about this as I do.' Whatever Henry's feelings on this particular subject, he continued to nod gratefully.

'Thank you,' he said. 'I might give her a ring later.'

'Do! I'll let myself out once I've rescued my sergeant.'

'When will they let me know about a funeral?'

Proby's eyes veered away, involuntarily ducking the other man's pain. 'I don't know. But I'll try to get you an answer as soon as possible.'

'I'd like to bury her as near Christmas Day as possible. She'd have liked that.'

Proby nodded and walked hurriedly out of the room. Not a naturally emotional man, he nevertheless felt tears coming to his eyes. To think of Anne, so lively, so ...

'I was that poorly, it was all catarrh, you see, thick gob, all down the back of my throat! So I said ...'

'Have you got that statement, Sergeant?'

Rootham leapt thankfully to his feet. 'Yes, sir. I've got it all down here. I've explained we're checking his shotguns, not that there's much point. It's a pity no one's invented a way of checking the provenance of pellets the way you can with a rifled bullet.' His voice had an uncharacteristic nasal sound. Perhaps he was catching a cold. They hurried out of the back door into the fresh air and made their way round the side of the house, through the gap in a thick yew hedge and back to their car, where the radio-telephone was buzzing angrily.

'What's up?' It was pleasant to hear Julie's soothing voice, pleasant also to catch something of her excitement.

'Oates says the Grogan girl's boyfriend has been lying. His alibi doesn't hold up.'

'That's ... let me think ... Hines. Jeff Hines?'

'Right! His mother said he was in all evening watching television. But one of the neighbours told Oates she saw him going out the back way just after the nine o'clock news.'

'And the time of the attack was put at ... ten forty?'

'He had plenty of time.'

'Somebody bringing him in?'

'They're on the way now.'

'We'll meet them there.' Even as Proby spoke, Rootham had sent the car accelerating down the driveway, turning on the twin blue flashing lights normally concealed within the radiator grill.

'Watch out for this black ice they keep telling us about!'

There was no reply as Rootham, his mind now concentrated on a new job, the job of reaching a suspected murderer and perhaps preventing a further crime, sent the car squealing round a corner and out on to the Bedington road.

'Alpha five?'

'We're on the A690 about ten minutes from Bedington.' Hickock sounded tense.

'Alpha nine?' A burst of static. 'Alpha nine?'

'Yrxxcz ... phleeep ...'

'Bloody things!' muttered Rootham. 'All this fucking technology, and it never bloody works when you want it!'

'Where's Oates?'

'Parked up your side of the garage.' Julie's voice returned, calm, reassuring. 'He's on Channel six–five.'

Proby jabbed at the buttons. 'Oates?'

'No worries, skipper! No one can go in or out without my seeing them. There's a big diesel wagon filling up now.'

'Who's serving?'

'I can't quite see. I think it's the father. Hang on! There's a car pulling in now. A big blue Jag. And there's a Range Rover coming up . . . Christ Almighty!! . . .'

'What? Oates! What? . . .'

'It's Doyle! There must be ten of them! I'm going in.'

'*Wait!*' More static. 'How far?' This to Rootham who had switched on the siren and was arching round a keep left sign straight into the path of an elderly van which sensibly took to the verge.

'Two more corners! Hold on! There they are! There's Oates!' Their car tore across the turf that separated the two carriageways of the bypass and bumped over the kerb, coming to a halt beside a mass of struggling men. As Proby leapt out, he could hear the thin wail of another siren approaching from the south. Somewhere in the seething scrum, someone was screaming.

'You just couldn't wait!' Proby sat glaring angrily at the composed, but bandaged, face of Hippo Doyle across the tin table of the little white-washed interview room.

The big man shrugged. 'He was lucky,' he said. 'Another minute, and I'd've done him.'

'As it is, you've broken both his legs, he's lost an eye and there's still not the slightest evidence that he did it. Where does that get you?'

'Back inside?'

The big man actually chuckled. Proby stared at him.

'You're lucky my young constable wasn't hurt.'

'He had a lot of bottle, coming in as he did.'

'You realize I can't interview Hines for at least two days. How does that help?'

'I feel a lot better!'

Proby raised his hands in despair. 'So how did you hear?'

Doyle smiled. 'You know me better than that, Inspector.'

'Take him back to his cell.'

Back to his office, Proby leant back in his chair and

51

watched two sparrows fighting over a piece of crust on the window-sill outside. Julie must have put it out for them. Actually there was no big mystery over Hippo Doyle's intelligence service. He probably just had a radio scanner permanently linked with the police broadcasts. Modern technology was neutral in the fight against crime, aiding the just and unjust alike.

He pressed a switch. 'I'll see Mrs Hines now.'

He was startled by the appearance of the woman shown into his office. Dark, slight, she looked no more than twenty.

'You're Jeff Hines' mother?'

She nodded listlessly. It was impossible to believe that the great bellowing lout they had bundled into the ambulance was this woman's son. For a start, she was so delicate, with tiny angular limbs and dark red rosebud lips.

'May I have some details first. Your full name?'

'May Hines.'

'Your maiden name?' He was fascinated by her ears. They were pointed, like a pixie's.

'Fattorini.'

'Date of birth?'

'What's this all about?' She lifted her head and stared straight at him. Her eyes were the largest thing about her, great black eyes with heavy lashes.

'I want to check your statements concerning your son's movements on Tuesday 12 December.'

'The night Mary died?'

'Yes.'

'What has my age to do with that?'

Proby met her stare. It was a fair point. 'There is some dispute about the evidence you gave then. I need your personal details.' It sounded thin even to him. But he wanted to know.

'I was born on 11 March 1962.' She was thirty-one, and her son was seventeen. She watched him closely. 'Satisfied?' She had a quiet voice, with an indefinable accent.

52

'Thank you.'

'It's the only thing people are ever interested in,' she went on. 'Would you like to know what he weighed?' Proby shook his head. 'Or what it felt like, being raped by a stinking tramp, or being held up as a freak because I wouldn't kill my baby?' Her voice was still steady, contemptuous. 'Do you know he may lose his sight completely?'

'I'm very sorry.'

'He was terrified of violence. We get enough of that at home. He'd no more have killed Mary Grogan than me.'

'Why did you lie?'

'Shouldn't you be cautioning me?'

'I just want to get at the truth. If your son did it, he can't attack anyone else in his condition, but if he didn't . . .'

'*If he didn't!*' she screamed, standing up, tears spilling down her cheeks. 'Have you *seen* what they've done to him?' Abruptly, she sat down again. 'I'm sorry,' she said. 'What were you asking me?'

'The night Mary died. You and your husband told my men that Jeff was at home with you, watching television.'

'Yes.' She seemed completely calm now, almost uninterested. The sparrows had gone, and a large coal-tit was tapping on the window with its beak.

'He was seen climbing over the fence at the back of your property at nine-twenty-five, or thereabouts.'

Her lips curled, less in a smile than a sort of sneering rictus. 'If Mrs Corrigan spent less time snooping, her husband might spend less time pestering others.'

'Nevertheless . . .?'

Her dress was so thin, he could see the line of her ribs.

'My husband was, as usual, dead drunk. I knew Jeff had been out. He likes wandering down by the gasworks. I think it's a roots thing. It helps him.'

'Does he know his father?'

'Of course not. I've never seen him again after that night. I used to dream about it every night. Now I don't suppose I'd recognize him if he was in this room.' There was something maddeningly passive about her now, as if she had had her outburst and no longer cared.

'Why didn't you have enough faith in him to tell us the truth?'

'Because I knew Reg, that's my husband, would take a stick to him just for being out. He hates him.'

'How long have you been married?'

'Fifteen years.'

'Your husband adopted your son?'

'That was the price,' she said simply.

'The price?'

'For fucking me! He wanted a schoolgirl. And that's the way I've had to stay. To keep my side of the bargain.' She was tired now. 'Jeff's just a big baby. He can't even defend himself against my husband. He just lies there whimpering and takes it; you saw him today.' She stood up. 'I'd like to go back to the hospital now. You've got the wrong man.'

Proby didn't contradict her, standing politely as she was taken from the room by an inquisitive-looking Hickock. As a matter of fact, he felt pretty tired himself. He didn't fancy facing Sheila either. What he did want to do was to get away and think.

Chapter 9

'Are you sure he won't disturb us?' Henry Bryant was sitting in Proby's fireside chair, looking up at Sheila. She was leaning over him, her face flushed with desire.

'Of course not. He's out chasing his precious murderer.' She stopped, appalled. It was, after all, Henry's wife who had been the last victim. Her lust had brushed everything else aside. But if Henry felt any incongruity in their conversation, he gave no sign of it.

'Well, if you're sure . . .' He picked her up.

'I'm very heavy,' she whispered delightedly.

'I'm very strong,' he replied, and indeed he must have been, because he carried her up the staircase and into the bedroom, throwing her squealing on to the bed.

'Now!' She opened her arms to him but he grasped her dress with both hands and tore it lengthwise so that it fell open, revealing the bruises of their last encounter.

'I need you.' She was tugging at his trousers, her fingers slipping on the greasy zip. 'Oh!' He had pulled off her tights and buried his head between her legs even as she pulled his trousers free of his boots. 'Oh God! *Oh God!!*'

'Do you like that?'

'Yes!'

'And that?' His voice had thickened.

'Yes!'

'And this?'

She screamed and pulled him round so that she could feel his weight on her. 'Now. Oh now. NOW!'

*

55

'I'm so sorry.' She lay cradled in his arms, the soft palpitations in her belly having long since banished her burning bursting contracting need to envelop him.

'Why?' He was staring at the ceiling, hardly breathing.

'I didn't mean to come so soon.'

'It was good.'

'And you?' She felt young again, shy and vulnerable in this violent man's arms.

He sniggered. 'Can't you feel?'

She gave an answering chuckle, 'I certainly can!'

'I'd better be going.'

'Yes.' Utterly replete, this time she did not contradict him. 'Yes, you'd better.' And it was only as she watched him carefully buttoning up his trousers that she suddenly thought of Anne, whom she had counted as a friend, then so briefly weighed as a rival, now so abruptly dead. Should she have shown more sympathy, felt more guilt? A dull pain alerted her to the bruises on her thighs. She didn't want to admit she was glad of the discomfort. At least it shows I'm human, she thought, and opened her arms to him as he came back for a final kiss.

After she had stood in the wintry twilight, watching his car lights disappear round the corner by the post office, she hurried back indoors to remove any signs of their encounter. First she ran upstairs, flung open the bedroom window and pulled what little was left on the bed on to the floor, bundling the bedclothes into her hanging cupboard and fetching clean sheets and a duvet from the little airing-cupboard behind their bathroom. Having remade the bed and changed the pillow-cases, she skipped downstairs again, tidied away the two wine glasses, and emptied the rest of the bottle of Chianti that Henry had brought down the sink, before carrying the bottle itself out to the bin-bag for bottles beside the garden door. That done, she returned slowly upstairs. Hugging herself she entered the bedroom, closed the window and then lay down on the bed, rolling this way and that, a wide smile fixed upon her face.

At last she heard her husband's car being manoeuvred into their garage, and then the sound of his key in the lock. Pausing for one quick triumphant look at herself in the mirror on her dressing table, she straightened her new blouse, hastily fastening one stray button, and went to the top of the stairs.

'Is that you?'

He looked up anxiously, feeling a deep sense of relief and gratitude when he saw that she was smiling down at him. The house smelt deliciously fresh.

'Hello, darling,' he said. 'It's nice to be home.'

Watching him, she realized with a shock that never before had she felt more significant than her husband. It was not exactly that he overbore her, or belittled her part-time employment in Mrs Tremayne's antique shop. It was just that she had always accepted that the demands of thief-taking were naturally superior to those of, say, making marmalade. They had discovered quite early in their marriage that they couldn't have children and at first much of her surplus energy had gone into making a home for Jim. But once she had ruefully admitted that he was so easily pleased that the smallest sign of caring was sufficient fully to satisfy him, she had, perhaps unconsciously, ceased to try. A brief affair with Mrs Tremayne's son had frightened her by unleashing a sexual appetite unknown within the tender embraces of her husband. Since that time, she had had two other equally brief liaisons, both with men she hardly knew but whose lust for her lavish proportions had lit an answering enthusiasm for which they had been all too keen to cater. And now she realized that there was a deeper second cause and effect of these episodes, particularly with Henry. It was that her life was now more interesting, more complex, perhaps even more dangerous, than Jim's. So there was not a little vanity, and even condescension, in her smile as she tripped down the stairs and accepted, with every outward sign of joy, her husband's loving hug.

'Are we friends again?' he asked.

'Of course. Let me get you some whisky, and then I'll make supper. Sausages and bacon do?'

His face lit up. 'Yes please! I've had a dreadful day.'

'You go and sit down. Ugh! This jacket stinks. Let me take it. Go on! Settle down in your chair, and then you can tell me all about it.' Really, he was just a big child. Later she would make love to him, softly and lovingly, the only way he knew how, but in the dark, so he couldn't see the bruises and scars she bore so proudly from Henry's hectic invasions.

And as she listened scornfully to her husband's happy paroxysm, closing her mind to its unwelcome physical manifestations, elsewhere in the city Detective Constable Hickock was surreptitiously passing a thick envelope into the bony hand of George Pratt under the table where the two of them sat, ostensibly enjoying a coincidental drink.

'I'm risking my job in letting you have these, George.' The detective's voice was truculent, and slurred by too much beer.

'Yeah, well I got you a bit extra from my guv'nor.'

'You did?'

'There's a hundred and fifty in here.' A second, and smaller, envelope made the return journey.

'Fair dos!' Hickock raised his glass, slopping a little of the tawny fluid. The journalist, who had made one pint outlast five of his companion's, raised his more cautiously in return.

'And there's more where that came from, if you can give me anything really meaty.'

Chapter 10

'The Lord gave, and the Lord hath taken away; blessed be the name of the Lord.' The vicar, a fat man with a boxer's nose, was heavily muffled against the bitter wind. There were only four shopping days before Christmas now, and he would rather be scouring Hampton for a present for his sister than officiating at the funeral of some criminal's wife, when neither of them had set foot in his church, thank God. But Mrs Doyle's body had finally been released by the coroner along with Mary Grogan's, and it had been the wish of both families (in so far as Hippo could express a wish from the remand wing of Her Majesty's Prison on the eastern boundary of Hampton) that the two girls should both be buried at St Jude's, Graceby. For there Anne Bryant, their sister in adversity, would eventually be laid to rest, once her remains came to be freed from earthly bureaucracy. Hippo, handcuffed to a tiny warder so that the two of them looked like a cliché of a comic turn, stood staring down into the grave. Behind him, Mary's coffin was being prepared for its final descent. There were policemen everywhere, a big contingent of the Grogan family, several journalists and assorted sightseers. The forecast was for snow, but the heavy clouds raced through the sky, fleeing westwards as the easterly gale drove them headlong before it.

'Bit of a circus, isn't it?' Henry Bryant, fulfilling two roles as bereaved husband and observant church-warden, stood in the lee of the church beside Proby and Rootham.

59

The latter was talking into a pocket-sized radio-telephone to the men who were discreetly recording the congregation on video for later analysis. 'The funny thing is,' he mused aloud, 'I think Anne would rather have enjoyed being part of this. I can't think of anything worse! But she was naturally gregarious.'

'You're coping, yourself?' Proby, one eye on the crowd, felt the need to show concern for the other. There's a broad and indistinct area between acquaintanceship and friendship which sometimes leads to misunderstandings. Certainly, geographical proximity is an unreliable criterion for choosing friends, although a good one for identifying shared interests. These two men lived within a mile of each other, worshipped at the same church, and currently shared the same woman. Either might have said casually of the other, 'Oh yes, he's a friend of mine,' and yet they were not friends. A loud wail announced the interment of Mary Grogan. There was a brief scuffle as her mother threw herself onto the coffin, and had to be pulled out of the grave and away to her husband's car.

'People are quite extraordinary!' said the vicar, walking across Henry's lawn after the multitudes had dispersed. 'It was very different at Lodsworth. Very different indeed.'

'Come in and have a reviving glass of sherry.' Even Henry's appetite for reminiscences of Lodsworth, a distant parish abounding with everyday tales of titled folk, had been sated by six years as warden to Dr Philips. 'Inspector Proby is going to join us.'

'How very nice. And when may I expect to be burying poor dear Anne?' The vicar took his warden's arm and squeezed it.

'You'd better ask Jim.' They entered through the french windows of his study, where Mrs Bertram had nurtured a cheerful fire. Proby, who had gone round by the public road to check that all numberplates had been duly noted, was already standing beside it, holding a mug of something hot.

'Good morning again!' The vicar rather prided himself

60

on his bonhomie, believing it to be an essential buffer against the ills of the world. 'We were just talking about poor dear Anne's funeral, and wondering when it would be?'

'There's no reason,' replied Proby cautiously, 'why it shouldn't proceed very soon.'

'Before Christmas?' Henry brought the vicar his glass of sherry.

'Today being the 20th? That might be pushing it. It all depends on the coroner. But then there's her family . . .'

Henry shook his head impatiently. 'They'll fit in with us. Her father is too frail, anyway. Alzheimer's. My sister-in-law looks after him at home, but it's a terrible ordeal for her.'

'Dear Lady Caroline had Alzheimer's . . .' began the vicar, but his two parishioners were too experienced to allow him to proceed. Proby, suddenly noticing the clock on the mantelpiece, shook hands and hurried away, while Henry, draining his own glass, admitted that he was already late for getting back to the Ministry of Defence.

The next step for Proby was to interview the one man who admitted meeting Anne Bryant in the Claxby woods. Not only that, he admitted he had been carrying a loaded shotgun at the time. However, Tom Clark was employed by old Colonel Bridgeman as gamekeeper and it was therefore his job to patrol the woods against predators, whether human poachers or animal vermin, so he was not high on the list of suspects. A small, tanned, gnarled little man in his mid-fifties, with a long beak of a nose and two bright birdlike brown eyes, he received Proby in the brightly polished comfort of his cottage parlour with all the courtesy due from one senior professional to another. In some ways, their jobs were alike. Both worked to impose their law on essentially lawless environments, Proby among the mean streets of Hampton, Clark among the dark glades and coppices of the Claxby woods. If Tom Clark felt a sense of superiority over his visitor, it was perhaps because Proby could only seek to prevent or to arrest; Clark acted also as executioner where stoats, crows and even foxes were concerned.

'Tea?'

'That would be nice.' At a signal from her husband, Mrs Clark, a quiet plain woman with watchful eyes, hurried to the old-fashioned kitchen range, poured hot water from an ancient kettle into the heavy black teapot, swilled then emptied it into the sink and began to busy herself with the ritual of making her husband's tea. Proby tried not to stare at the two shotguns and light .22 rifle propped up against the corner of the stove. Of course they should be locked away in the now obligatory 'burglar-proof' cabinet. Equally, of course, a man of Tom Clark's generation wasn't going to change the habits of a lifetime. A terrier of great age lay snoring in front of the stove. From time to time, its legs quivered.

'How long,' began Proby conversationally, 'have you worked here?'

'All my life.' The little man's straightforward and appraising look was slightly unnerving.

'You came here from school?'

'I was born here. My father was head keeper to the Colonel's uncle. There were four of them in those days. Now I have to manage with just my lad.'

'Is that difficult?'

The terrier let out a shrill yelp in its sleep. Clark ignored it.

'No.' He shook his head. 'It's all very different, but we manage. I don't have the bother of rearing birds with broody hens. It's all done with incubators. And there's not half the trouble with poaching since they closed the Castlewick pits.'

'But...?'

'Well...' the master of the house watched as first he and then his visitor were served with tea, accompanied by thick slices of white bread heavily buttered, 'it's not the same now the Colonel lets the shooting. Mr Bryant's a nice enough gentleman, in his own way. But once these syndicates took over, well – ' he paused – 'it's more about numbers than sport, if you understand me?'

'Tell me about Mrs Bryant.' Proby was not in the mood for anthropological analysis. 'You met her that morning?'

'That would be the day she died?'

'Yes.'

'A nice lady.' Would he never get to the point? Proby took a sip of his tea. It was delicious.

'Where exactly did you meet her?'

'Let me see.' The gamekeeper cocked his head. 'I'd just trapped an old stoat down in the chalkpit by Midwinter's boundary, so I reckon I was coming up past the new planting when I first saw her.'

'Was she standing still or walking?' Proby could never escape a creeping feeling of excitement at the reconstruction of a crime. The sense of being there, even through the medium of another's evidence, made him feel close enough to be near the scent of his prey.

'Standing still.'

'In this weather?'

'It was cold, but it weren't raining. The woods looked a picture, with the frost on the boughs. Like today.' Proby glanced out through the little window. The view, out across a deep valley to the whitened woods beyond, was indeed idyllic.

'Could she have been waiting for someone?'

The keeper gave him a sharp look.

'I'd wondered that,' he said slowly. 'At first, I thought she was talking to herself.'

'Did she come often?'

'Once or twice a week. I couldn't be sure. We've still got six of the big woods left. Me and the lad spot most people, but you can't be everywhere at once.'

Proby smiled sympathetically. He often felt like that himself. 'Had you ever seen her with anyone else?'

'Apart from Mr Bryant?'

'Yes.' Again he cocked his head.

63

'No,' he said after a pause, 'no. Although she always stops and chats if she sees me, or the Colonel, or poor Luke, as found her.'

'Does Luke ever carry a gun?'

This time the keeper burst into a deep chuckle. 'It wouldn't do much good if he did. He couldn't hit a barn door, old Luke. The Colonel lets him come out on the cocks day. I lend him my Watson 12-bore,' he gestured at the armoury by the stove, 'but it don't do him any good.' There were tears of laughter in his eyes. 'I reckon Mrs Bryant would have been safe if Luke were after her.'

'Did she come on regular days?'

'You mean, could someone have expected her to be there?'

'Yes.'

He shook his head. 'No. No. I'm sure there was no routine to her. I asked Nat, my lad, that.'

'You seem to have thought a lot about it,' said Proby.

'Yes,' replied the other. 'This is my patch. And I don't like murder done. Least of all Mrs Bryant. A beautiful young lady.'

'You spoke to her?'

'Yes. I wished her the compliments of the season, and asked her if she wanted any pheasants plucked over the holiday.'

'And she?'

'She asked after Mrs Clark, and said how beautiful the woods were looking. She looked as happy as a lark.'

'Did you hear the shots?'

There was a long silence.

'No,' said the other at last. 'It's funny that. I went off to check my traps in Willoughby Wood, but I'd've thought I would have heard them. We get a lot of them helicopters over from Castlewick nowadays. I suppose that might have been the reason. There's that many, I don't notice them specially any more.'

He could easily have done it. He was on the spot. He was actually carrying a shotgun with the type of barrels envisaged by Ballistics. But why should he? Watching him, Proby guessed that he might kill a man with as little pause as one of his unfortunate weasels. Braithwaite had already established that both he and Luke the forester had been at home with their wives when Mrs Doyle and Mary Grogan had died. Whatever the solution to his problem, he was convinced it did not lie with this spry, efficient countryman, whose method of keeping order in his rural precinct was so admirably simple: a silent approach, a careful aim, the swift disposal of the body. No need for the rules of evidence, no risk of being confused by the deliberate trickery of smooth-talking barristers paid to help their customers escape the penalties of crime. Justice was done, and order prevailed.

In every case, there came a point when Proby wanted to escape, to get clear of procedure, to reflect. Where better than in the Claxby woods, the scene of Anne's encounter with her killer? Outside, he found Rootham, his nose streaming, chatting with Nat Clark, a fresh-faced youngster about the same height as his father but with his mother's closed, cautious expression.

'When you two have finished, I want you to find Luke and go over his story again. I'm going for a walk in the woods. We'll meet back here in, say . . . two hours from now.'

Rootham, all too used to his superior's whims, checked his watch and continued to interrogate the boy.

Striding down the muddy lane that led past a high hedgerow into the valley, Proby began a detailed review of the case. The mud was frozen, making the ruts hard to walk on. The small shoots of winter wheat that punctuated the field seemed dwarfed by the great clods of solid clay. Everywhere the frost had outlined even the most fragile tendrils with silver, repainting the dun-coloured landscape of winter with a glittering palette. He had been born in just such a setting. Goonby-in-Farthingdale, the little village where his mother had been schoolmistress while his father kept the post office, had sat squat and defiant in the wilderness of the Yorkshire dales, buffeted by the storms of youth. Had the winters really been more severe in those days, or did his memories of long weeks of snowbound isolation stem from a child's imagination given authority by passing time? A black cock pheasant rose with a raucous cry from almost beneath his feet, skimming away across the stunted grass, a sudden burst of exotic colour with angry slashes of maroon and mauve among its dark feathers.

Now he was inside the wood. He paused and sniffed the air. Snow was coming. He could sense Nature's anticipation of the approaching change. The whole wood seemed tensed and silent, waiting for its magical transformation. Was it a path like this, winding between the crisply iced bracken, that Anne had trod? What was the real significance of the three murders? What had these women in common? Why should anyone want to kill them, without apparently pursuing either rape or theft? Somewhere, deep in the wood, he heard the harsh cry of a jay. He stopped, pulled out a packet of cigarettes, and placed one in his mouth. For all Sheila's distaste, the evidence would be long gone by the time he returned home that night. Cupping his hands, he flicked a match and applied it to the tip. The unexpected result was to make him cough. Angrily, he flung the smouldering cigarette over his shoulder, and walked energetically up the ride. Somewhere quite close at hand he heard the sharp explosion of a shot, followed by another. Pigeons . . . or young women? He ducked through a thick belt of black pines, following the direction of the shots without regard for paths. The brambles clung to his trousers, and he could feel an icy dampness penetrating his shoes. His breath turned into mist around him – it was coming harder, in painful pounding gasps. Was he getting too old for this sort of thing? The excitement in his head told him otherwise.

'Who the devil are you?'

Proby had burst through another frozen thicket to find

himself facing a tall bent old man with a red nose, dressed in faded oilskins, and carrying a shotgun. His moustache, white and droopy, was so large as to appear at first sight to be false. The man sounded angry rather than frightened – but then, of course, he had the gun.

'Inspector Proby, Hampton Police.' The old man nodded, apparently satisfied.

'I've got a bird down here somewhere,' he said vaguely. 'I don't suppose you can see it?' Proby gazed about vainly, repressing the desire to ask if they were looking for a blonde. 'And I've lost my dog!' The old man had a long whistle, made of brown horn, suspended round his neck on a length of orange baler twine. He blew rather helplessly into it, but without result.

'You haven't by any chance seen Clark about?' he asked.

Proby nodded. 'Yes. He was in his house half an hour ago.'

'Idle bugger!' said the old man. 'He knows we've got to thin out these damned pigeons. They're eating all the pheasant feed, you know.' He nodded his head violently.

Proby couldn't take his eyes away from the moustache. It was magnificent.

'Are you Colonel Bridgeman?' he asked, having already deduced the answer.

'I am,' was the reply. 'And I'm delighted to see you here. I know we don't get the gangs we used to when the pits were open, but that doesn't mean Gaffer Gaught has carte blanche to snaffle my pheasants. I'm very glad you're taking it seriously at last.' He pulled out a large red and white spotted handkerchief, and wiped first one eye and then his nose. 'I've got a stinking cold, you know,' he said. 'That's the worst of this weather, you can't shake 'em off.'

'I'm actually here about the woman who was murdered.'

The old man assumed an expression of great gravity. 'Yes,' he said, 'of course. I was very shocked to hear about that. I knew her, you know. Anne something-or-other.

67

Pretty girl, wife of the chap who takes the shooting here. When you get to my age, one name means much the same as another. Though I wouldn't forget yours. I had a friend at school called Proby. Peter Proby. No relation, I suppose?'

Proby smiled and shook his head. He wasn't sure his father had been to any school, let alone one likely to have produced Colonel Bridgeman.

'I was away that day, so I'm afraid I've got an alibi.' The old soldier chuckled. 'I was up in London having my hair cut, and if that idiot Soames can't see anything else, he can certainly see well enough to make out his bill!'

'Soames?'

'The barber. Bloody man! It takes three hours to get there, three hours to get back, and he nearly cuts my ear off!' And indeed it was true. His right ear had a distinct gash, partly concealed under a filthy piece of old Elastoplast.

'Did you often meet Mrs Bryant . . .'

'Bryant! That's the name! You are clever.'

'Did you often,' pursued Proby doggedly, 'meet Mrs Bryant in these woods?'

The old man looked thoughtful. '*There she is!*' he shouted. '*Here!*' and blew piercingly on his whistle. An enormously fat black Labrador came waddling up the ride, a half-eaten pigeon carcase sagging out of one corner of its mouth. '*Look at that!*' he shouted above the wind. '*It's not as if we starve her at home!*'

'Did you often meet Mrs Bryant in these woods?'

'What?' The Colonel cupped his hand to his ear. 'What's that you say?'

Proby leant towards him. '*Did you often meet Mrs Bryant in these woods?*'

'No,' laughed the Colonel. He actually raised his free hand and stroked his moustache. 'I'm far too old for that sort of thing! I say, there's Clark now.' And indeed Proby had already seen the purposeful figure of the little game-keeper striding towards them, a gun under one arm and a sack over his shoulder.

'I must be getting on,' the Inspector said.

'Don't forget what I said about Gaffer Gaught,' said the Colonel. 'Thirty years he's infested these woods. It's high time he was behind bars.'

When Proby reached his car, Rootham was already at the wheel, talking into the telephone.

'It's Hickock at the hospital. They say you can talk to young Hines now.'

'Tell them we'll go straight there now.'

Chapter 11

The main hospital serving Hampton was split between two sites, on either side of the Castlewick road leading west from the city centre. On one side rose the seven-storey tower of glass and concrete raised in that confident age when health spending seemed the ultimate sacred cow, a god whose appetite had always to be satisfied however gross. Because the medical team whose priorities had dictated its design had long since been replaced by new men with different requirements, the building contractors had never actually left, with the result that although the Children's wards, Ear, Nose and Throat, and Maternity units had indeed been installed there, along with Mental Illness controversially sited on the top floor, the Accident and Emergency unit was still crammed into the temporary wartime huts erected across the road beside the old Portland stone County Asylum, a distinguished eighteenth-century building which housed the offices of the various health administration units.

'Park the car and join me at the desk.' Proby got out of the car and walked over to the main door. An ambulance had just drawn up outside, and an old woman, evidently with a broken leg, was being stretchered into the building by the ambulance crew. She was also very drunk. Across the hall from the reception desk was a small kiosk, staffed by a St John's Ambulance team, which sold flowers, magazines and chocolates to the passing trade. Casually he bought an evening paper and opened it up,

'NEW CLUE IN MURDER HUNT!' screamed the

banner headlines. 'LOVE LETTER CACHE
REVEALED!' And a sub-heading: *'Who is the mysterious Mr "S"?'*

Proby swore loudly. He read:

Today the *Gazette* can exclusively reveal the existence of a major new clue in the hunt for the Hampton Maniac. A cache of steamy love letters, addressed to the late Mrs Diana Doyle, murdered wife of gangland czar 'Hippo' Doyle, throws new light on the series of savage murders currently paralysing our city. Although these letters came into our hands anonymously, and contain passages that cannot be printed in your Favourite Family Newspaper, we have taken the unusual step of reproducing parts of the letters below to recruit YOU THE READERS in the hunt to find this lunatic-at-large. Before he kills again! (Hampton CID and Detective Inspector Proby PLEASE NOTE!) We have taken this step, supported by legal advice from our PEOPLE'S ADVOCATE, in the public interest. If you can identify the writing of 'Mr S', ring Mandy or Sharon on HAMPTON 4000, and we will rush you a bottle of your favourite bubbly!!

And indeed, below this effusion were reproduced facsimiles of two of the letters with appropriate passages blacked out.

'George Pratt!' muttered Proby under his breath.

'How much?' Rootham had joined him unnoticed.

'Look at this!' Proby thrust the paper into the other's hands. 'So much for security! And I haven't even had the graphologist's report yet.'

'Julie says it's on your desk. Came in the second post.'

'Bloody woman! Why couldn't she have delivered it?'

'Julie?' Rootham sounded shocked.

'No! The graphologist. She only lives in Stanbury.'

'Here's Hickock.'

The older detective, looking decidedly hung over, was crossing the reception area towards them. 'Shall I lead the way?' he asked.

Proby handed him the paper.

'What do you know about this?' he asked sourly, but with no particular suspicion. Unfortunately for Hickock, the effect of an evening's tour of his local bars coupled with a guilty conscience wrote his involvement in block capitals all over his pale perspiring face.

'Me?' He hadn't even glanced at the paper.

'I see,' said Proby drily. 'We'll talk about this later. In the meantime, let's be seeing what's left of Jeff Hines.'

The fat young man was in a bad way. Both legs were in plaster, as was his right arm. His head was thickly bandaged, and a drip feed was attached to his left arm at the wrist. His bare neck showed some angry abrasions, and his mouth seemed oddly swollen. The nurse who had been sponging his neck stood up when the three policemen entered. She glared at Proby and left.

'Hello, Jeff.' It seemed rather an inadequate way of greeting a man he didn't know, and who couldn't see him.

'Who's there?' The voice was surprisingly high-pitched for so bulky a source.

'I'm Detective Inspector Proby and I've got two other officers with me.'

'Was it you pulled that bastard off me?'

'I'm sorry I didn't get there sooner.'

'You and me both! I've lost my right eye, did they tell you that?'

'Your mother told me.' The boy didn't reply. He must be nearly eighteen, thought Proby. As fat as a pig. There was an odd sound from the bed. Could he be crying under all those bandages? 'We've got the men who did this,' he added. 'They'll pay.'

'Man,' said the boy. 'It was that big bastard. The others just held off my dad, and the lorry driver. I reckon he's crazy.'

Proby found himself wondering whether the boy had inherited his mother's ears, underneath that mass of bandaging.

'Why didn't you tell us you went out the night Mary died?'

'You didn't ask me.'

Rootham silently handed Proby the boy's signed statement.

'It says here,' said Proby, reading. ' "I stayed upstairs all night after an early supper with my mum and dad, playing with my computer, and watching a Val Doonican tape." ' The figure on the bed started to shake his head, and stopped abruptly. 'That's the statement you signed for DC Oates.'

'Yeah, well, my mum had made her statement, hadn't she? I couldn't contradict her, could I, not with Dad in the room. He doesn't like me much.'

'Violent, is he?'

'I thought so until I met this geezer.'

Proby smiled. If the boy could make a joke out of a situation like this, maybe he'd still make something of his life. Clearly he had inherited his mother's grit.

'So where did you go?'

'Where I always go.'

'Which is?' Somewhere a bell was ringing with shrill persistence.

'Do I have to tell you?'

'Yes, Jeff, you do. This is a murder inquiry. There aren't too many secrets in a murder inquiry.'

'Except who dunnit!'

Proby was beginning to like him. He laughed; the other two stared at their superior as if he'd gone mad.

'So?'

'Does my mum have to know?'

'I shouldn't think so.'

'What does that mean?'

The nurse put her head round the door. She was young

73

and black, with angry eyes and a broad unsmiling mouth, with a mole at one corner.

'Haven't you finished with him?' she asked. 'He needs rest.'

Hickock, desperate to rehabilitate himself, went to eject her, but Proby forestalled him. 'I'm sorry, Staff,' he said. 'But this is important. If I think he's flagging, I promise I'll send for you.'

She left the room without replying.

'Now then . . .'

The boy still hesitated. 'Can I tell you on your own?'

'Certainly.' Proby gestured to the others, and they left the room. 'They've gone,' he said.

'Straight up?'

'Yes.'

'I went to Kenneth's.'

'I see.' Proby kept all inflection out of his voice. Castlewick's only gay bar was five miles in the opposite direction from Hampton. The boy probably had a better alibi there than at the family garage.

'I like to keep my life private.'

'We all do,' said Proby soothingly, but couldn't resist asking, 'And Mary?'

'Mary was a good friend. She understood. I could talk to her. Not my mum, though. She wouldn't have understood.'

Nor would her husband, thought Proby.

'You won't tell no one?' The bell in the distance had started to ring again.

'I promise you.' Proby leant over and laid a reassuring hand on the boy's good shoulder.

'Thanks.'

There seemed nothing more to say. Proby let himself out silently, passing the nurse as he did so. She had nothing to add either. The bell continued to ring.

'You got the wrong lad, Hippo.' He had stopped off at the prison on the way back. A great castellated gate led into what looked like nothing so much as a series of

74

tall out-of-date factory mills. The chief warder, Robin McLean, was an old friend of Proby's, tall, white-haired and ready for his retirement. He didn't believe in rehabilitation, having seen too many of his poor misunderstood guests returning again and again to share the unsavoury atmosphere, one part urine to three parts sweat, in which his whole working life had been spent. They didn't learn better, he was fond of quoting, they only learned more. Hippo was a good example. This was his fifth visit to Mr McLean's establishment, and the low-ceilinged chamber where the three of them now sat was familiar to them all.

'So you say.' The big man had indeed lost a lot of weight, and his blue shirt clung to him, with dark damp patches on his chest and under his arms.

'The Governor's very put out,' said McLean. 'He thought Hippo was a reformed character.'

'You and I know better, Mr McLean,' said Hippo, with a show of his dreadful teeth. 'But we mustn't tell him it's no good, must we? It'd spoil his appetite.' The warder rolled his eyes. Between the warders and the governors in the prison service is a truly cavernous chasm fixed. 'So who do you think it was?' This last was addressed to Proby.

'We're working on it,' Proby replied. 'We'll catch him.'

'It won't bring my Didie back.'

'Nor Jeff Hines' eyesight.'

If Proby wanted a show of remorse, he was disappointed. Hippo shrugged. 'Filthy little faggot!' he said. 'I'd do the same again for fun.' As Proby got up to go, Hippo called out, 'By the way, Mr Proby! When can I have my letters back?'

Proby stopped dead. 'Your letters?'

'Yeah. I wrote some kinky letters to Didie. Just for fun. Used to get her in the mood, like. She was a right little monkey in the sack!' In prison he seemed to have reverted to the sort of cliché-talk he obviously felt was expected of him. Even his voice was lower, his accent more exaggerated.

'And how did you sign these letters?'

75

'S for Sexy.'

Proby laughed.

'I'll see you get them tomorrow,' he said. And left with a broad grin on his crinkled face, to join Rootham and Hickock who were waiting outside in the car.

Chapter 12

'The writer of these letters is male, aged between twenty-nine and sixty-three with a pronounced tendency to violence.' This was the hand-written précis which the graphologist retained by the Hampton police had inscribed on her seventeen-page report. Proby flung it into his paper-bin with a chuckle. There was a knock on his door and Hickock sidled in. He did not look happy.

'How much did George Pratt pay you?' snapped Proby, all trace of his good humour effaced.

'Pay me?' asked Hickock desperately.

'Listen to me.' Proby looked his subordinate up and down.' You were a good detective ten years ago. I know, because I chose you for my team.' The other made to interrupt, but decided against it, biting a fingernail instead. 'Ever since you and Beryl broke up, you've gone from bad to worse. You drink too much, I've had two complaints of sexual harassment, you were lucky to escape with a reprimand over the Winston Roberts case, and the only time I raised the question of your promotion with the Super, he told me to leave comedy to the experts on the box. Now you've taken to nicking confidential material and selling it to the press.'

'You've got no proof of that,' said Hickock sullenly.

'No,' said Proby, suddenly angry, 'and if I had, you'd be out of this building this evening. So let's hope he paid you enough to take the place of your pension. Because one step out of line, and it'll be a fond farewell. Is that plain?'

Hickock stood up. 'You shouldn't speak to me like this,' he said.

Proby looked up at him, and the other dropped his eyes. Proby sighed. 'I'm having you transferred. You'll be re-assigned next week. In the meantime, take two days off. I don't want you cluttering up my investigation.'

'Which is such a success!' sneered Hickock, and walked out of the room, slamming the door. A few minutes later, Julie came in carrying a steaming mug of coffee. She smiled at him.

'I know,' she said. 'I shouldn't be performing menial tasks. But I thought you'd like this.' She put it down beside him. 'I debated whether to ask the Chief Superintendent to bring it in for you, he being the only other officer on this floor at the moment, but after careful thought, I decided I could risk being gender-stereotyped just this once!' He found himself beginning to relax. 'That's better,' she said. 'I gather "Groper" leaked our letters?'

Proby shrugged. 'It didn't need a detective to work that out.'

'What does the graphologist say?'

He grinned ruefully. 'It came too late to be relevant. I got a confession.'

Her face was a picture.

'You what?'

'Hippo,' he explained. 'He just mentioned it casually this afternoon. All that work, and if I'd asked him in the first place, he'd have told me he wrote those letters to titillate his young wife!'

'They were a bit saucy,' she admitted. 'I rather liked them myself.' Their eyes met, but so fleetingly that the atmosphere remained light.

'I must go home,' he said. 'Can you double-check Henry Bryant on the PAN computer program? I couldn't get it to come up with anything under him at all. I must have keyed something in wrong.'

'Have you done your Christmas shopping?' He shook his head. 'You do know tomorrow's Christmas Eve?' He'd completely forgotten!

'I'll get something for Sheila before I come in. Who's minding the shop tonight?'

'Geoff Milbanke.'

'Tell him to ring me at ten tonight. I want him to keep me in touch.'

She nodded, watching him hurry down the corridor before turning out of sight through the staircase door. In February, when her promotion came through, she would be working on another team. The more she thought about it, the more she realized she would miss his benign bear-like presence.

Outside the air was, if anything, slightly warmer. Proby's car, a red Saab, was parked in its designated space in the underground garage. He drove home slowly with the roof half open, sniffing in the pure wintry air, wondering when the snow would come.

Sheila met him at the door, and hugged him with unexpected fervour. 'How nice you're home.'

He buried his face in her hair, then turned away and went over to his desk. 'Did you go to the shop today?' he asked brightly.

'No,' she said, laughing. 'You know today's my day at home. I've had a lovely time, having a really good go at the kitchen before Christmas.'

'Any visitors?' Very lightly phrased.

'No,' she said, 'thank goodness. That's the last thing I needed, I can assure you!' She laughed joyfully.

He watched her in the mirror, sadly coming to terms with a situation he had had to face before. Her hair stank of cigar smoke. She was lying about her day. She was, he deduced, being unfaithful. And as before, he minded dreadfully. It didn't need an immense leap of intuition to place Henry as most probably the lucky recipient of her affections. No wonder she had been startled at the news of Anne's death? He wondered how long it had been going on.

'Macaroni cheese?'

He dredged up an enthusiastic exclamation – traditionally this was a special treat for him. He might prefer it not to have been earned through Henry's caresses . . . He stopped. I must not jump to conclusions, he told himself. An affair, yes. But Henry is not the only man who smokes cigars in Hampton. And yet he knew.

'How's the case coming along?' she inquired brightly at the kitchen table. He was forking out the remaining crust of baked cheese from the rim of the dish.

'Slowly,' he said. 'Too slowly.'

'Any firm suspects?'

'Half a dozen,' he said cautiously. One of Sheila's invariable giveaways was her need constantly to bring her lover's name into the conversation. This was in fact the way he had learnt about her first lapse, although he had never given the least indication, then or later, that he had known.

'I suppose,' she mused, 'even Henry Bryant must be on your list?'

'I'm afraid so,' he said, munching thoughtfully. 'Being the husband automatically puts him in pole position.' He tried a light laugh. She didn't join in. 'Ridiculous, isn't it?'

'Ridiculous!' She slopped some more wine into her glass.

'That was delicious,' he said, standing up and taking their plates over to the sink. 'One of your best.' The odd thing about her affairs was that they always made her more uxorious rather than less. He had hardly started on his mug of tea when she grabbed his arm impulsively and, dragging him to the sofa, proceeded to display a bewildering intensity of passion. Why did he stay? Why was a man so aggressive in enforcing the law so passive in his emotional life? Did his very impassivity invite these situations?

He had first met Sheila on a murder case. She had been the secretary, and probably the mistress (they had never discussed it), of a middle-aged gunsmith with a shop in Mayfair. He'd been seconded to the Met and when the gunsmith had been found, minus head and genitals, locked in the boot of his Bentley in the long term carpark at Gatwick, he'd been given the job of investigating Sheila. When they'd caught the villains almost immediately, the gunsmith having been part of a ring smuggling arms to Rhodesia, Proby was halfway through his investigation. They finished it together in bed, and married six weeks later after his promotion came through. He was thirty-two and she was only eighteen; he'd spent most of his life north of the Humber, she'd been to fifteen countries with the gunsmith but never ventured outside the North Circular; he was tall and obsessively fit, she was voluptuous and the only exercise she ever took was in bed where, she said, she did try to make up for not wasting his money in the gym. They'd been married now for twenty-three years, no children, no rows and, increasingly, no communication. If she wanted a fling with Henry, was it really such a disaster as to wreck their relationship? Was sexual exclusivity the irreducible minimum that one creature must demand of another in order to live together?

She might have bloody washed her hair, was Proby's grumbling thought as he poured himself an unaccustomed slug of whisky from the unopened bottle they'd brought back from Florida in February. They were due to go to Australia this coming year, but that would have to be postponed if the young ladies of Hampton were still being peremptorily despatched by his anonymous prey.

'I'm going to have a shower,' she said, gathering her scattered clothes in an untidy bundle, and coming over to claim another kiss. Her green eyes held no expression at all. 'You look very romantic!'

He realized to his chagrin that he was still wearing his shoes and socks.

The door bell gave its regulation jangle. Sheila shrieked and ran up the stairs. Proby grabbed his shirt and began to pull it on with one hand, while trying to get his trousers over his shoes with the other. The bell rang again.

'I'm coming!' he shouted. A fist began to pound on the glass. His shirt was inside out. He went to the door.

'Who is it?'

'Rootham. There's been a reported attack down in the sidings.'

'Give me two minutes!'

Chapter 13

'What happened?' Some time that evening, the promised snow had begun to fall. The streets had turned from hard-edged skating rinks etched with sharp black shadows into a soft snowscape blurred by drifting flakes. Indeed there was a disturbingly mesmerizing effect as the whirling snow, flickering white and blue with the reflection of their lights, seemed to rush towards them out of the darkness as Rootham sent the car slithering through the dead-ened suburbs.

'He botched it!'

'Another girl?'

'Yeah, but it seems she slipped as he fired, and what's more there were a couple of drunks nearby. They chased him off.'

'Did she get a look at him?' They had to swerve to avoid an abandoned car, one wheel sunk in a pot-hole, the sidelights still burning.

'The local copper said she was too shocked to speak. This was twenty minutes ago.'

'Cordons in place?'

'Just as you ordered.'

'Can't this car go any faster?'

'Not if you want to arrive the other end.' A cat appeared in their lights, its angry eyes flashing a reflection as it paused fastidiously with one paw raised before bounding into the black shadows. Proby pressed some buttons on his pocket phone.

'Hello?' There was a crackle. 'Is the Chief Constable

in, please? ... I see ... What? ... When do you expect him home? ... Thank you.' He turned it off. 'Dining with the Lord Lieutenant,' he commented. Rootham did not reply.

In the days when the docks had thrived, so too had the railways. The goods that flooded out to equip the Empire converged from north and south and east along the three great metal tracks that met at Hampton, providing ceaseless employment for those who brought them there, those who transferred them into the waiting ships, and those who accompanied them out of the estuary on their various exotic routes. And of course the same process could be carried out with matching profit in reverse. Now that most trade went by more modern routes and its other customer, King Coal, was in as much decline as the national dynasty, the huge delta of old water-meadow, carefully drained and reinforced by the Victorian engineers to cater for the three railway companies, was now a wasteland of rusting metal, though still owned, fenced and theoretically patrolled by British Rail. In all nearly 200 acres, it was crossed by two living lines, the mainline London route and the smaller local line along the river valley, taking in Castlewick, Bretby, Snarlston and (eventually) Huddersfield. Two footpaths, heavily fenced with razor wire, crossed this bureaucratic rubbish heap, and they met at a four-way metal bridge known locally as Fusilli Junction, on account of its many rickety spiral staircases. Much of the fencing, and almost all the arc lights, were out of commission, so the place had a violent reputation for crack-dealers and muggers. As the great expresses thundered through and the local trains shunted this way and that with no apparent sense of urgency, there were only two reasons why a girl would be there on her own: drugs or prostitution, probably both.

'How far now?' He knew perfectly well. But he was so tense now, already in the mind of the killer, out there somewhere in the snow, with a shotgun and the knowledge that it was he (or she) who was now being hunted.

Would he go to ground? Or make a run for it? A large shape loomed up immediately in front of them, causing Rootham to brake so hard that the car slewed round and skidded into the kerb.

'Christ!' said Rootham. 'They've brought old "Self-ridges" out of store.' It was the Incident Truck, a brain-child of the Deputy Chief, vast, unwieldy and packed with equipment more suited to a thermonuclear attack than a simple case of murder.

'There you are!' Detective Chief Superintendent Rankin had been on holiday when the first murder was committed. Now he was back, and though thoroughly content to leave the case to Proby, a chance to see the investigation in action gave him an excuse to escape the stifling conditions that accompanied Christmas as cele-brated by the Rankin household. 'We've got your young lady in here.' He was tramping up and down, dressed in a leather jacket with a heavy fur collar. One end of the forty-foot articulated lorry had been turned into a secure interview suite complete with taping facilities, surveillance chamber and the latest gadgetry available to those with access to the public purse. Climbing the carpeted steps and passing into the inner room, Proby found a very thin girl of about nineteen being comforted by a uniformed nurse who was standing beside Julie. She had a bandage over one shoulder, and seemed dressed in rags. In another part of the suite, he could hear shouting.

'Hello,' he said. Julie winked at him.

'This is Lomi,' she said. He pulled up a chair.

'You've had a lucky escape.' The girl just stared past him. She was clutching a cup. She had large almond eyes and smudged lips painted scarlet. Thick black mascara had run from her eyes. She looked a mess.

'My name's Jim.' Should he treat her as a child? If he had had a daughter, she'd be the same age as this waif. The girl let out a thin disconcerting whistle.

'Lomi!' She looked at him. He saw something very familiar. It was fear, fear not of crazed murderers brandishing shotguns, but of all-powerful interfering officials.

'I'm a policeman chasing a murderer,' he said. 'I don't care if you're an illegal immigrant. I don't care if you're on the game, and I don't care if your pockets are stuffed with dope.' She didn't look as if there was space for a pocket anywhere. 'I need to catch this killer. You're the only one who can help me.' There was no sign of outrage, other than from the nurse, who had made a sucking sound through her teeth when he mentioned immigration. 'So tell me what happened.'

There was a long, long silence.

'Would you rather tell Julie here?' No reply.

Would you rather I beat it out of you? he thought, but stayed silent, watching her gaze flicker towards the nurse and back.

'Would you mind leaving us alone, nurse,' he said with the nearest he could get to a charming smile. She gave a shrug and walked out. Julie closed the padded door.

'He was tall,' said the girl. 'I couldn't see his face. He had a scarf pulled over it. He wore a white raincoat, and a tweed cap. He was old.'

Proby sat back in his chair. The perfect witness!

'Are you sure it was a man?'

She paused to think. 'Yes. The way he walked.'

She was wearing a cheap scent. It made him want to sneeze.

'You're quite sure?'

A sardonic smile came and went. 'I know how men walk.'

Julie laid a comforting hand on hers. Unexpectedly, he could hear people singing. Loudly and very out of tune.

'How old?' She looked him full in the face, appraisingly. Would he ever reach the stage of needing sex so badly as to pay this child or someone like her? 'As old as me?' She smiled. She was missing several teeth.

'No,' she said. 'Perhaps forty-five?'

'Where do you live?' All the animation left her face. She stayed silent, as if she hadn't heard. He sighed. There were more important things to do. 'Julie,' he said, 'you explain to our friend Lomi that her life is in very considerable danger, and that whatever her circumstances she will need to be in protective custody until we find this bastard.'

Outside in the trailer corridor, the singing was louder.

'On Mother Kelly's door . . . step,
Down Paradise Road . . .'

Young Braithwaite came out of another door, grinning from ear to ear.

'Look,' said Proby angrily, 'I know it's nearly Christmas, but . . .'

'It's the hoboes,' said Braithwaite. 'They saved her life.'

'Did they see him?'

'Average height, white coat, two heads.'

'Great!' said Proby. 'I can just imagine the scene in court. Let's get out there. That's where I want to be now.'

Less than five hundred yards away, Henry Bryant crouched in the roof space of a derelict goods van. His shotgun lay beside him, dismantled now into three pieces, the stock, the barrels and the eighteen-inch hinged buttress-piece that joined them together. His white raincoat, detached now from its reversible leather lining, was already cut into small strips, ready for burning. He was wearing a shabby dinner-jacket. Beside him lay a large jack-knife, a revolver, his cap, gloves, a shabby white bundle of material and a thick grey scarf, all placed carefully on the oilskin wrap in which he carried the gun.

Through the thickening snow, he could see a policeman below him, stamping his feet. Several others could be heard moving from truck to truck. Thank God they had no dogs yet! But first he had to go home. They would certainly check his movements, and for the story to fit, he needed to reach his car within two hours. He checked his watch: 9.43 p.m. He was completely calm. Having been hunted by EOKA in Cyprus and the CBV in Berlin, the prospect of evading a scratch posse of Hampton bobbies held few threats. It was all a question of time. They were searching the second class carriage on the next siding. What simpletons! He pulled out his cigar case, smiled to himself, and put it back. There was no point in deliberately courting disaster. Nor did he particularly want to have to shoot his way out. He checked the extra box of bullets in his pocket. More voices, and nearer now. He picked up the revolver and checked the safety catch. The voices stopped. The body of the van vibrated as the guard's door was dragged open. He could see the gleam of a torch.

'Any tracks?' It was Proby's voice.

'No, sir. We reckon he's wearing snow-shoes.'

'If it would only stop snowing for half an hour, we'd have him.'

'Of all sad words of tongue and pen, the saddest are these: it might have been!' quoted Henry to himself, with a sardonic smile, three feet above their heads.

'We need more men. I want this whole area sealed off until morning.' The voices began to move on. The policeman outside followed them, thus saving his life. Time to go! Henry pulled on the brown lining, after first carefully packing the shotgun's pieces into a roll that attached to a stout belt. Removing the two boards that had led to the refuge he had prepared some weeks before, after choosing this particular site among others. He waited patiently in the dark of the van. Two minutes, one minute. He could hear his rescuer coming, miraculously on time. The silky white bundle opened out into a camouflaged boiler suit, with a long zip up the front and elastic at the wrists and ankles. Calmly, he adjusted the hood. As the mail train, its rusty lights twinkling through the blizzard, shuddered and slowed at the points beside his van, waiting for the down express, he slipped across in its shadow, and swung himself under the bogey. Four minutes later he was being carried over the Castlewick Road crossing, only feet away from the boots of two disgruntled constables, called out from their warm beds to spend a freezing night watching for a man who never came.

Henry's car, artistically entombed in a snowdrift just north of Claxby, was only five minutes' walk even in those conditions from a steep incline on the railway line where the mail train had to slow. Scrambling down the embankment, he replaced his snow-shoes and made his way as quickly as he could across the shimmering fields. He approached his car cautiously, along the line of a tall hedge. There was no one about. Nor had anyone disturbed the threads laid across the doors. So far, so good. He opened the door, and taking off the white boiler suit and what remained of his coat, he thrust them and both guns into a hinged space behind the door panel. Pulling on a heavy woollen overcoat, he got into the driver's seat, started the car and drove slowly home, missing one of the Chief Constable's drink-driving patrols by a matter of seconds at the Stockard St Peter crossroads.

It was snowing even harder now. He parked at the back of the house and checked the time. Allowing himself ten minutes to prepare, he walked into the house. Less than that, and his story would be that he had intended to dine with friends but got stuck in the snow. Longer, and he had never set out. It was a standing invitation, and he had deliberately left it open. First he checked his ansaphone. Nothing. Then he ran upstairs to shower and change while the television recorder was rewinding. Refreshed, but still ready for the police check that he knew must come, he fast-forwarded the evening's programmes, noting their salient points while downing three large glasses of neat whisky, a drink he abhorred. Already feeling unsteady, he walked round to the back of the house to check that the tracks of his car were well covered. They were, and the engine was so nearly cold that his mind consciously changed gear. If they came now, he had spent the evening in. He brought the gun in, carefully rodded it through, and left it on the table. This was not bravado. He had been flighting pigeons earlier in the evening as an elementary

89

precaution against the paraffin test. He always left his gun out. He was keeping to his normal routine.

In fact, it was nearly eleven before the unfortunate Sergeant Milbanke, theoretically in charge of base operations, had to be reminded by an angry, cold and exhausted Proby to check on their only real suspect who wasn't in either prison or hospital. Proby came himself, hammering on the great oak door with unusual vigour.

'Jim! Come in.' Henry stood swaying in the doorway, his smile loose but welcoming.

'Have you been out tonight?' Proby's eyes strayed to the gun on the hall table.

'No. But come in. You're letting the snow in!'

The detective had no choice. Uncomfortably aware of Rootham, as wet and tired as himself but sitting out in the car, he followed Henry into the warmth of the study.

'I'm on the hard stuff. I got frozen up in the woods this afternoon.' Henry waved his glass. He stank of whisky. 'Let me give you some.' He slopped it into a tumbler, spilling some of it. Proby took it in silence. 'Do you know,' continued his host, 'this will be my first Christmas without Anne. The very first.'

'I'm sorry,' said Proby. 'We nearly caught him tonight.'

'There was a piece about you on the news,' said Henry. 'You looked very po-faced, I thought.'

Proby grunted, taking a swig of the whisky. 'Anybody been with you tonight?' he said.

'Who the *fuck* do you expect to be with me?' Henry sounded fighting drunk. 'I've lost my *fucking* wife. What do you mean, bursting into a man's house and asking a question like that?' He stood up. 'Get out! Go on, get out!'

Proby rose. 'I'm sorry,' he said. 'We need to check these things.'

'Get out of my house!' Henry was beginning to enjoy himself. Perhaps the whisky had been too clever a ploy. But Proby went quietly, hunching himself against the driving snow that was already half-obliterating the police car.

'Well?' He was back in the car.

'His engine was cold,' said Rootham. 'No sign of tracks, but then there wouldn't be. It's a two-edged weapon, this weather. Aren't you taking him in for a paraffin test?'

'Hmm. No point.' Proby was staring into the storm. 'He had a gun out on his table. He'd only say he'd been out in the woods shooting pigeons. It's what he did say, in fact. The funny thing is, that's the first time I've ever seen him the worse for drink.'

'Drowning his sorrows?'

'Maybe.'

'You reckon he's our man?' asked Rootham, sensing the other's mood from long experience.

'Of course he is,' said Proby. 'But catching him's another matter. Let's go home.'

Chapter 14

It was nearly noon the next day before they found the guard's van with the loose boards. Proby pulled the men away immediately until the forensic technicians could get to work.

'We should have had dogs. It was my fault.'

'There wouldn't have been any scent,' said Rootham soothingly.

'To think he was just above our heads!'

'And us unarmed!'

Proby nodded. 'Even so, we'll never get another chance like that.'

The whole of Hampton, city and countryside, was smothered under a sparkling blanket of new snow. The sky was clear now, and a pale wintry sun won answering flashes off the clear waters of the estuary and the frosty windows of skyscrapers alike. It was a day for brightness. Christmas Eve, and the snow in the streets was trampled into slush by the busy anxious crowds hurrying from one shop to another in search of last-minute needs. Mollie Rootham, weighed down with a fifteen-pound turkey, struggled into the patisserie for a quick cup of tea, only to find Sheila tucking into a mound of Black Forest gateau.

'Can I join you?' Thankfully she slung her plastic bag underneath one of the little cane chairs. 'Where's Wendy?' Instead of the brisk young redhead who normally presided, a short dark man had sidled over. He had a printed plastic card which announced 'Hi! I'm Stefan!' and closely set brooding black eyes.

'Just tea for my friend,' said Sheila, speaking rather loudly and slowly as if the man was either deaf or mentally defective. 'Isn't it awful,' she whispered as he waltzed away, 'it's under new management. I hate changes, don't you?'

'I wonder where Wendy's gone,' mused Mollie. 'She was such a nice girl.'

'So what have you got there?'

'This?' Mollie gave the bag an unenthusiastic dig with one aching foot. 'That,' she said, 'is our turkey. Fresh from Mr Monck.'

'Here we are, ladies.' The little waiter managed to make the word sound like an improper suggestion. He winked and let out an alarming bray of mirthless laughter.

'Am I going mad, or has he got an inordinately large bottom?' hissed Sheila after he had turned his attentions to another couple at a distant table. 'Who on earth is that tart he's talking to now?'

Mollie turned round. A young woman with bobbed fair hair and bright pink lipstick was listening to the waiter. Her companion, an older woman, looked highly unamused.

'Gosh, you mustn't say that!' she said, turning back. 'That's Julie Birch, the office angel. She works with Jim and my Ted. I think that's her mother. I've seen them together before.' With another of his loud unmusical laughs the waiter minced away, revealing a tall glass animal that stood on the table between the two women. From a distance, it seemed to be an elephant, or perhaps a rhinoceros. It looked very expensive.

'They're welcome to her,' muttered Sheila, who was in a bad mood because her cocoa had come with insufficient sugar. 'I missed our weekly do together.' It had been cancelled because of pressure of work for their husbands.

'Same here. Ted says it's only a matter of time now.'

'Why? What's happened?'

'You must have heard about last night.'

Sheila gave a snort. 'I'm the last person Jim would tell.

However, to be fair, I was asleep when he got back, and he'd gone out again before I woke this morning.'

Mollie, who'd stayed up to give Rootham his cough medicine when he got in, and had set the alarm to cook him a proper breakfast before he went out again, looked at her companion with surprise. Did she play no part in her husband's life at all? There had been rumours, as there always were. Some computer salesman, and one of the Tremayne boys. Even so. Perhaps it was she, Mollie, who was the freak, mothering her husband instead of getting on with her own life?

'They nearly caught him!'

'I thought they said it might be a woman.'

'No longer. Three people saw him. I think . . .' Mollie lowered her voice and leant towards Sheila, 'but you mustn't say I told you this, I think they know who it is!'

'No!' This was real news. 'Who?'

Mollie shrugged. 'Ted wouldn't say. He's maddening like that. But that's the impression I got – a very clear impression in fact.'

'Look at that tart!' The couple across the way were leaving. 'She's wasting her time wiggling her hips at our Stefan!' They both giggled companionably. Catching the sound of their laughter, the little waiter approached.

'Yes, senoras? How may I please you?' The little eyes were cold, a killer's eyes.

'The bill please.' Rather reluctantly, Mollie picked up her massive burden. Her feet were wet and sore.

'When do we meet again?'

'Next Wednesday, I hope.' said Sheila. 'Merry Christmas!'

'Merry Christmas!'

In his office three streets away, Proby sat waiting for his appointment with the Chief Constable. He was not looking forward to it, despite his Superintendent's unequivocal support. He had spent the morning carefully analysing all the facts of the case, aided by the reams of thermal paper that had spewed out of his fax machine from the National Analysis Bureau now based at the new police computer block in Gravesend. And as he did so, with reluctant clarity, he saw a pattern. What was worse, he saw the face of the murderer. In acknowledging this, he was tacitly acknowledging that he had known all along. Diana Doyle's murder could have had any number of explanations: a vengeful husband, a taunted lover, a rival competitor of her husband's rackets, or just a common or garden roving maniac. Mary Grogan's death statistically narrowed the field to a maniac or a man with a plan. Anne's lonely death, for his money, brought it down to the man with a plan.

For all their seeming isolation, the Claxby woods were actually quite secure. At the very least, the murderer was a man (or woman) who knew the Claxby woods. Rootham was out with Braithwaite now, trying to trace the old poacher, Gaffer Gaught. Anne being the only woman regularly to be found there, whereas the other two women were among hundreds who might be found walking on the towpath or in the docks, it followed that Anne at least was probably a deliberate target. And if Anne was the target, Henry was the front runner for no subtler reason than that he was her husband, such being the melancholy statistics of family death. And if Proby knew of no reason why Henry would wish to kill his wife Anne, he knew the man enough to be able to accept that if it were to be done, it would be done efficiently and with careful forethought. But to slaughter two innocent young women? It would be going too far to say that Proby was a slave to his intuition. He had been wrong before, but he was more often right. Drawing on his cigarette, he blew out a deeply satisfying plume of soft smoke. So! He had wind of his prey. But how to prove it? And would Henry try to strike again, to deepen the public perception of a serial lunatic? Perhaps not, after last night's debacle. At last his telephone rang, and he started his long walk up to the seventh floor.

'The Chief Superintendent said you wanted authorization for a full Section 53 surveillance?' The Chief Constable was also suffering. He had a bottle of pills in front of him, together with a bottle of something thick. He blew his nose loudly and then peered cautiously into the handkerchief, staring at whatever lay there with fascinated concentration.

'Yes. On Henry Bryant, the husband of the third victim.'

'Henry Bryant?'

'Yes, sir.' The Chief Constable stared at him.

'You know he's number two at Castlewick?'

'Well, I knew he worked there.'

The Chief Constable snorted. 'I should think he does. He's their head strategic planner for overseas operations for a start.'

'Does that make a difference?'

The senior policeman examined the contents of his handkerchief again. 'We'd have to involve Special Branch,' he said. 'Are you sure you want to do this? He shoots with the Lord Lieutenant, for God's sake! Where's your evidence?'

'He has no real alibi for any of the shootings. He owns a shotgun. He was married to the third victim. He has no alibi for her murder. I believe he killed all three to divert attention from the murder of his wife. The evidence of our only reliable witness fits, but would be inconclusive. I'm sure he's our man.'

The Chief Constable sat back in his chair and gazed at Proby. 'And the motive?'

'I don't know.'

'You don't know! So what it comes down to is this: here's a man with an unblemished, indeed distinguished reputation, a very senior Government official, a man with everything to lose. You have one husband, a man with a massive criminal record, into every sort of violence, locked up for GBH and you have a second man in intensive care having lied about his alibi. But you want me to support an application to put a full monitor Section 53 into action against the first man?'

'Yes, sir.'

'On a hunch?'

'To stop him murdering again.'

'It's not good enough. I can't possibly support this. The Home Secretary would have a fit. You've got no evidence, no motive, and most people think it's a casual maniac. You said so yourself the other day. Good heavens! The man's church-warden in your own parish!'

'I really think we should keep an eye on him.'

'Oh God,' groaned the Chief Constable, eyeing the medicine bottle with a vindictive glare. 'Are you really going to make an issue of this?'

'It'd look very bad if he killed again, sir.'

'It'll look very bad if you're wrong.'

Proby smiled. He could identify a threat as easily as any man. 'Thank you, sir,' he said, judging it better to assume his superior's support rather than continue to discuss it. 'After all,' he added as an afterthought, 'it shows that we're pursuing every possible avenue.'

'Yes, yes.' The Chief Constable had had enough. 'I'll speak to the Home Office. This sort of thing costs a fortune.'

'I don't believe you!' Sheila, only her head emerging from the dense aromatic foam, sat facing Henry in the deep bath. He had telephoned her as soon as she had returned from the shops, and she had joined him, waiting in a side street until she had seen Mrs Bertram cycling home. 'He can't think you did it!'

'He does.' Henry smiled across at her. 'Can you pass me the soap?'

'But why?'

'Because you have made me delightfully smelly.'

'No, not that – why does he suspect you?'

'Statistics. Most wives are murdered by their husbands.'

She smiled back at him. 'There are times when I wouldn't mind murdering him,' she replied.

'There you are then.'

'Be serious.' She gazed lovingly at his long eyelashes.

Suddenly she realized why sex was so good with him. She wanted his baby! She'd never felt like that before.

'I could see it in his eyes,' he was saying. 'It's part of my job to recognize that sort of thing.' I want his baby, she was thinking: a little baby boy! 'Are you listening to me?' She nodded mistily. 'We can't go on meeting.'

'*What?*'

'Well, not for a little bit,' he added hastily, shocked by her violent expression. 'He's bound to put me under surveillance. Luckily, I'm all too familiar with the ropes, but we'd be caught out straight away, and that would look very black against me, wouldn't it?' Tears were pouring down her cheeks. 'Wouldn't it?' he persisted. The water surged in the bath, slopping over on to the thick carpet as she launched herself into his arms, regardless of the tidal wave she was causing.

'I can't live without you,' she cried. 'I love you!'

'And I love you,' he replied, trying not to think of the delicate stencil-work on the ceiling below. With luck, the water would be absorbed by the carpet, or trickle away down the wall cavity. 'Just for a little while. But,' he added, holding her by the shoulders and forcing her to look him in the face, 'there is something you can do for me.'

'What?' she said eagerly. 'What can I do?' Unconsciously she was already re-creating her relationship with her husband whereby she had subordinated her interests completely to his.

'Try to find out what he's doing. It will make it easier for us to evade them. I need you so much!'

'Oh God how I need you!' she wailed.

Heedless of the stencil-work below, he heaved another wave of water on to the floor by shoving her up against the end of the bath and giving her convincing proof of his continuing affection to the accompanying sound of slapping water. Come to think of it, he reflected as he watched her carefully repairing her make-up at Anne's table, a week or two under surveillance might prove something of a relief.

'See you tonight,' she said, interrupting his train of thought.

'Tonight?' He'd thought he'd just warned her off for weeks!

'The Midnight Service, silly. You'll be on duty, won't you?'

'Of course.' He smiled at her, relieved. 'Take care.'

'You too.'

It was nine o'clock that night before the necessary authorizations were in place, and not before the Chief Constable had had to cope with indignant calls both from the Defence Ministry and, later, from the Home Office. Watching well back from within a darkened bedroom, Henry smiled grimly as two unmarked vans were manoeuvred discreetly through the snow into place at either end of the street. He knew now that his telephone calls would be recorded. Very likely a strong directional microphone would be used tonight until the inevitable unscheduled visit tomorrow gave them access to the house. He would be followed by four teams, working round the clock. What a lot of money to spend on one harmless man! Who would come tomorrow? Christmas Day. The gasboard? Proby himself. His shotgun was now back in its rack with the others. The coat was burnt, along with the gloves, cap and scarf. They had been specially bought for the job, and had never come into Mrs Bertram's sphere of influence. He walked downstairs, took a fresh cigar from the box on his desk and sat down beside the fire. There was just time to finish *Robinson Crusoe* before he would have to start getting ready to walk over to the church for the service.

Chapter 15

In the little church, Dr Philips was carefully sorting out his box of hymn number-cards. There were, he noticed, several missing. But tonight he would need more Ones than usual, because the Christmas carol sheet went no higher than nineteen. They would start with 'Once in Royal David's City' for the procession. Not that St Jude's gave him very much scope for processing, having a short chancel, no side aisles, and an even shorter choir that ended abruptly with the uncompromising bulk of the heavy Victorian altar. Anyone taking the liberty of swinging a censer could hardly avoid laying one or more of the congregation out cold. How very different it had been at Lodsworth where even the side aisles had had side aisles, and the great church had positively reeked of incense. At least no one here wanted him to transgress in the direction of the 'Alternative' services. He had two wardens, Henry, appointed by himself, and Ruth Carpenter, an excellent woman who ran the travel agency in Hampton, appointed by the Parochial Church Council of which she was Chairman. By common consent, they kept to the King James version, though allowing themselves a little latitude as far as the official revisions were concerned.

'What weather!' It was Ruth Carpenter herself, stamping her boots on the vestry floor. She was a tall woman, with a long jaw and wispy grey hair imperfectly gathered into a bun.

'Do you think it will affect the congregation?' The vicar helped her remove two coats, a scarf, a quilted waistcoat and a coarsely knitted fisherman's jersey.

'Oh no!' she said stoutly. 'It takes more than a little snow to deter our people!'

The next arrivals were the elderly organist, the crucifer and Henry, followed almost immediately by two young men in donkey jackets and jeans. The vicar eyed them anxiously.

'They must be the new family on the estate,' he whispered to Ruth.

She stared at them. 'One of them appears to be listening to his Walkman!'

The vicar shook his head in disbelief. A single woman now entered. 'Who's this?' he muttered. And suddenly the church began to fill. The Bertrams, all fifteen of them, occupied the last five pews on the north side, then several couples heavily muffled, even old Colonel Bridgeman, in a brown herring-bone suit and a red and yellow striped tie, coughing loudly and smiling roguishly at the single woman. Henry was busy handing out the hymn-sheets and prayer books, wincing slightly as fresh gusts of snow preceded each new arrival. The service was due to start at 11.45. With two minutes to go, the door opened and the Probys slipped in.

'Here you are.' Henry slipped the books into Sheila's hand while smiling at Proby. 'A proper white Christmas!'

'Yes indeed,' replied Proby, matching his smile and carefully avoiding the temptation to glance at the other detectives. Would they know how to behave in church? He led Sheila up to the second pew, the only one still empty. With a congregation of nearly seventy, the little church presented an image of serving a community that had changed little over the past century. The previous Sunday services had netted a combined total of eleven. The expanded suburb surrounding them housed nearly seven thousand.

'... therefore with Angels and Archangels, and all the glorious company of Heaven...' On his knees, uncomfortably aware of increasing pain but unwilling to forgo his ritual obeisance, Proby watched the vicar and Henry preparing to administer the sacraments. On busy nights, like now and Easter, one of the wardens was recruited to serve behind the altar rail. Out of the corner of his eye, he could see Sheila's lips moving earnestly in prayer. What must her thoughts be, beside her husband and about to receive the Communion cup from her lover's hand? He risked a glance backwards. The plainclothes men were watching events by the altar with expressionless faces. The girl from Special Branch appeared to be asleep. She'd been flown up from London by helicopter, a dangerous journey in this weather. She looked too young to be out of school, with her pale skin and long bleached hair with its modest black Alice band. He turned back to find Henry's eyes disconcertingly fixed upon him. What lay behind that ironical, almost teasing expression? He lowered his head on to his hands, and tried again to compose a worthwhile prayer. Peace? Goodwill toward men? He'd be quite satisfied with Henry behind bars. Somehow that seemed an inadequate, even blasphemous detail with which to trouble the Supreme Being on the anniversary of His birth. And yet, when he thought of the suffering of Mary Grogan's parents, the agony in Hippo's eyes, Anne Bryant's lonely Calvary, why not ask for help in preventing further suffering? He couldn't himself solve the world's famine but, with God's help, he might bring peace to Hampton's pedestrians. 'Please God,' he found himself praying, 'help me catch this man, whoever he may be.'

'Are you going up?' Sheila was jogging his arm impatiently, and Ruth Carpenter, whose job it was to usher up the communicants in due order, was standing beside her.

'Yes,' he said. 'What about you?' She shook her head, avoiding his gaze. Squeezing past her, he joined the queue.

'The body of Our Lord Jesus Christ . . .' He cupped his hands and felt the vicar place the wafer, a snapped morsel since supplies had been found inadequate, in his palm. Gratefully he consigned it to the roof of his mouth.

'The Blood of Our Lord . . .' He couldn't bear to look up at Henry, but took the chalice firmly and drank. The message of Christmas was, he found, in no way diluted by coming by way of a source he believed to be tainted. Deeply refreshed, he walked back down the chancel steps, to be met by a knowing wink from the Colonel who was strolling up in his turn.

'Only decent service in the district!' Had he imagined the words from under that majestic moustache? Nevertheless, it reminded him that no one had yet made contact with Gaffer Gaught.

For the final hymn, the old organist sprang to life and the beautiful tune which he had not heard for exactly twelve months swamped the building. They all stood:

'Christians awake! Salute the happy morn
Whereon the Saviour of the world was born!'

Above the strange warblings of his neighbours, two of whom sounded distinctly drunk, a magnificent soprano voice soared out, clear, ringing, even in tune.

'To Christ our Saviour and the Virgin birth!'

Several people turned round. It was the Special Branch detective, Mary or Mamie, he had hardly heard the introduction, muffled as it was as they crouched beside the listening van. What a voice! Why hadn't she sung out before?

He turned and saw the answer. Her face was transfigured. She might have entered this little building, a heap of stones piled one upon the other when Chaucer was a child, in the guise of a professional police agent, intent upon spying. But now she was a simple Christian, proclaiming her faith in the best way she could. Again he caught Henry's eye upon him. Catching the Colonel's mood, he winked, and was rewarded by a look of consternation crossing Henry's face. It was Christmas morning, for all the grim rage of the tempest outside, and Proby was determined to celebrate.

Chapter 16

This festive mood evaporated, however, when Sheila and he exchanged gifts the following morning. As usual, she had given him a present apparently designed more for communal than for personal use. On opening the mouth of the opaque plastic bag which served as wrapping, he found a cardboard box with the blazon 'Kaffee Freund'.

'It makes cappuccino,' said Sheila helpfully. 'I'm afraid they didn't have one in stock that made espresso as well.' He smiled – last year it had been a waste disposal unit – and hurried off to the coat cupboard where he had concealed her present the night before.

'Here you are,' he said, diffidently producing a big square parcel elaborately wrapped in a paper that sparkled with a red and gold zigzag pattern secured with white ribbon.

Sheila raised her eyebrows. 'Did you do this?'

'Look inside.' She tore off the wrapping and ripped open the lid of the sky-blue box. Inside stood a tall glass elephant. He watched her expectantly. She turned, walked up to him and hit him hard across the face. The last woman to hit him had laid his chest open with a machete before Rootham had got her in a neck-lock. This time he was on his own.

'What was that for?'

'If,' she spat, 'you can't give me a present without getting your floozie to buy it for you, I'd rather you gave me nothing at all.'

'At least I don't fuck her!'

As soon as he'd said the words, he regretted them. She blushed scarlet, her whole face suffusing with angry blood, even her eyes seeming to fill with crimson tears. When she ran at him, he was ready and held her sobbing and struggling, while she choked and snarled at him, in a way so entirely foreign to the suppressed inversion of their normal intercourse that for a moment he thought she was having a fit.

'Let go,' she said, suddenly calm. 'Let go of me, please.'

He released his grip. 'I'm sorry, I shouldn't have said that.'

Her face was completely blank. It was as if she had been embalmed. 'How did you know?' Her voice was flat, without colour. She was looking at the floor, one hand massaging the other wrist.

'My darling.' He went to hug her, but she flinched, turning away to evade his tentative embrace. 'If you want to conceal your affairs, stick to non-smokers.'

'Affairs?' This time her eyes, blue and cloudy, rose to meet his. Her nose was running.

'Henry is number four? Or number five?'

'Four,' she said flatly. 'I didn't know you knew.'

He shrugged his shoulders. 'I'm a detective.' He tried a little smile. Miraculously, she smiled back. 'That's better,' he said incautiously, as immediately the smile faded.

'Don't patronize me,' she snapped. 'I hate it. I always have.' Then unexpectedly, 'Shall I make you some coffee?'

'Only if it's black,' he said with a sad sense of irony at the expense of the intricate, but to him useless, piece of engineering on the table. She nodded and disappeared into the kitchen, leaving him to survey the wreckage of Julie's skilful wrapping. How could Sheila have known? 'Married to a detective' would no doubt be her response. She came back with two mugs, black coffee for him, milky for her.

'Let's talk,' she said, and sat down heavily on the sofa, but in such a way as to prevent him from joining her.

'Okay,' he replied, perching on the arm of a chair and placing his mug carefully on the little table beside him.

'If you knew about them, why have you stayed with me?'

He'd sometimes wondered that himself. 'I don't know. Because I love you.' Was her stare contemptuous? Could love only be seen as a weakness to those who stood outside its protecting walls?

'You can't love me if you know I'm being unfaithful to you.' She made it sound like one of Life's eternal truths.

'Why not?' He tried not to look at her breasts, which were accentuated by the tightness of her jersey dress.

'You fancy me,' she said. 'That's all.'

'Yes,' he said. 'I do.'

'Don't you wonder why I've done this?'

'I imagine it's my fault. Everyone knows being married to a policeman is no fun . . . I'm often away . . . it's not unique.'

She glowered at him, this handsome, calm, infuriatingly kindly husband who still managed to drive her into other men's beds. It wasn't that he was a bore, it was just that he made her feel so pointless, not by being unkind, but by placing so much emphasis on his job.

'Stop being so PERFECT!' she said. 'It's very irritating.'

He laughed. 'I'm sorry,' he said. 'What would you like me to say?'

'I think I want to marry Henry.'

He was shocked. 'Has he asked you?'

'Of course not.'

'Did you ever sleep with Vernon Andrews?'

It was her turn to be taken aback at the mention of the long-dead gunsmith.

'Why didn't you ask me at the time?'

'Did you?'

'Of course I did!'

'And what can Henry give you that I can't?' He was expecting the answer 'passion', but instead she said softly, 'He makes me feel guilty.'

'Guilty?'

'Mmm. Can you understand that?'

The telephone rang. It was Rootham. 'Is that you, skipper?'

'Yes.'

'You told me to ring you.'

'I know. Get on with it.'

'The listeners are all in place.'

'Anything interesting?'

'Not yet. That bird from London's a bit special!'

'So's your Mollie,' Proby reminded him. 'Happy Christmas.'

'Happy Christmas,' chuckled the other and hung up.

'I want to go on talking,' said Sheila, 'but first I must see to the turkey.'

Henry had been right to expect a visitation. In the event it was indeed two gas board engineers investigating a fault in their system.

'Such are the blessings of privatization,' he told them with a straight face. 'I've never seen a gas man working on Christmas Day before.' They smiled politely. He gave them plenty of opportunities by going across to the church several times, and then amused himself by guessing the places they had hidden microphones. The telephones were, of course, obligatory. He was unimpressed by the bedroom light and the kitchen clock, but gave them full marks for the cavity behind the bathroom stopcock. It was just the place he would have chosen himself.

Chapter 17

'Don't you want to watch the Queen?'

Proby looked at his watch. It was nearly three o'clock. They had been talking for almost five hours, with a short break to eat their turkey.

'Yes, I do,' he said, ignoring her satirical expression. An ardent, some would say fixated, royalist, he really looked forward to his annual address by his sovereign. Turning on the set, he saw the familiar face swimming into focus.

'Many of you will feel as I do,' she was saying, 'that our Commonwealth, with its great traditions of tolerance and racial harmony, with its inter-continental tapestry of hope woven on the loom of generations past, whose warp is experience and whose weft is compromise . . .'

'What?' Someone was shaking his shoulder. It was Sheila, Sheila smiling!

'You were asleep,' she said. 'Ted Rootham's here. There's been some trouble.'

He jumped up. Rootham's face was strained.

'It's that Asiatic girl,' he said. 'She's dead!'

Looking down at Lomi's peaceful face, it was impossible to imagine the devastation that lay at the back of her head, where the bullet had struck. Braithwaite's story was a simple one. He'd been by her bedside in the private room off Ward C at the hospital when the fire alarm had gone off.

'Was it snowing?'

'You know it was snowing! It's been snowing for two days!'

'Was the window closed?'

'Yes,' said Braithwaite, his face tight with anger and shame. 'The window was closed.'

'So you went out into the corridor?'

'I heard Tom Oates shouting. I took my gun and opened the door. That's when he fired.'

'Through the window?'

Braithwaite shook his head. 'No. That's the funny thing. He must have opened the window. From the outside.'

'It's not difficult if you know how.' Proby examined the old wartime catch sourly. 'How could he have known she'd be here?' The young detective shook his head again, the picture of frustrated self-reproach. 'What happened then?'

'I didn't realize for ten, maybe twenty seconds what had happened. She never made a sound. The shot sounded miles away. Then I saw the blood on the opposite wall.'

'And . . .?'

'I ran to the window.' He pointed out hopelessly. 'You can see for yourself. It was useless. I radioed Oates and did what I could for the girl. She was already dead.' He sat down and leant his head against the wall. There was more shouting outside. To Proby's surprise, he suddenly found himself staring into the reddened eyes of a massive Alsatian which was standing on its hind legs looking in at the window. Abruptly he pulled the flimsy curtains across. They did not meet, allowing anyone to see the inside of the room with perfect clarity. He touched the radiator. It was red-hot. A scared nurse looked in.

'Are you Mr Proby?'

'Yes.'

'The Chief Constable's outside.' He walked out into the corridor.

'I thought this was the sort of thing you were supposed to prevent?' The Chief was wearing a grey suit, with a red flower in his button-hole. 'I take it your suspect is in the clear?'

'We're checking now, sir.'

'A fine way to celebrate Christmas!'

'I agree.'

'Where's the Chief Superintendent?'

'On leave in the south, sir.'

'Is that man ever on duty?' There seemed no safe reply to this so Proby stayed silent. 'Oh well...' the Chief spotted his reflection in the corridor mirror and carefully removed the flower and stored it in his pocket. 'This will need some explaining.' He walked away down the corridor to where a television crew were testing their lights. Proby returned to the little room that already smelt of death. He sat down to wait for Dr Milligan.

'Let me hear those tapes again.' There were five of them crowded round the amplifier in the van, Proby, Rootham, Maggie from Special Branch and the two technicians, both older men with matching moustaches.

'That's the television.'

'Can you hear him moving?'

'No.'

'Try the bathroom.' One of the technicians turned a knob. Another tape on the broad face of the machine began to spin.

'What's that?'

'He's flushing the toilet.'

'Time?'

'The man consulted a dial. 'Eleven fifty-seven.'

'Nothing since then?'

'He was in the kitchen at 1.05, and again at 1.17.'

'Basting the turkey?' Nobody smiled.

'Who've we got outside?'

'I've got it down here.' She really was amazingly young. Proby watched her flick through her notebook. 'Reynolds and Hall took over at noon... they were the two in church last night.' He nodded.

'How much could they see in this weather?'

'Precious little,' she replied. He had had to walk up from the bottom of the hill having left his car by the post office.

'Could he have got out?' he asked.

'Easily.'

'Easily?' He was astounded. What were these people paid for? The van was shaken by a particularly vicious gust.

'I think you and I had better talk,' she said, with a self-possession he found rather annoying. It was not that he was unused to being lectured by a woman, it was her assumption that he was missing something that irked. Outside, the storm was worse. A strong wind blew the snow through their clothing, and it was impossible to make themselves heard above the blast. Somewhere he thought he heard a tree falling. Bent double they made their way through the deepening snow down to his car. Rootham had left the engine running, so it was warm inside though still noisy as the tempest rocked the car. They were less than three hundred yards from Proby's home.

'My boss isn't pleased with you,' she said with a smile.

'Why's that?'

'Mr Bryant's by way of being a bit of a special case,' she explained. 'He wrote the definitive textbook for fieldwork in Counter-Espionage. If you're right, and no one thinks you have a shred of real evidence, we've as much chance of containing him covertly in visibility like this as you have of stopping this storm. But it's an intriguing challenge.'

'This isn't a game,' he protested. 'Four women are dead.'

She nodded. 'I know. He won't strike again.'

'Why?' He felt foolish even asking.

'Because he's achieved what he set out to do, which you are assuming was to kill his wife. Everything else has been to deflect suspicion, not very effectively it has to be said.'

The car telephone began to buzz.

'Proby.'

'We've had the lab report.' Julie's voice sounded bored.

111

'The bullet came from a .38 handgun, range about 4 metres. We have no record of its markings on the computer.'

'Interpol?'

'Geoff's accessing their files at the moment.'

'Thanks.' He turned to the woman beside him. 'This is where you can prove your worth. Take his house apart, and don't come out without a .38.'

'We won't find anything,' she said. 'I've been to his lectures.'

'Just do it,' he said, and filled in the blank warrant he had obtained earlier in the afternoon before struggling back through the storm to give it to Rootham.

When he joined them, the house was in turmoil. There were eleven of them at work, with two dogs. Henry was sitting in his study, whence the aromatic scent of Cuban tobacco announced his pained acceptance of the inevitable disruption. Holloway from Forensic came out to announce sotto voce that the firearms test was negative. 'Not that that means anything nowadays,' he muttered. 'He could easily have been wearing a PVC covering.'

'Is that you, Jim?' Henry had come to the door leading into the hall where his three shotguns were being carefully wrapped up for inspection at the Groby Road laboratory.

'Sorry about this.' Proby went over.

'My dear fellow! I quite understand. But what has happened to precipitate all this . . .?' He gestured at the chaos around them. One man was methodically taking up the floorboards, and from somewhere upstairs came the sound of glass breaking.

'Another girl's been killed.' There seemed no reason to lie.

'And I'm your only suspect? I must say,' he added with a twinkle, 'I don't feel very much like a raving homicidal lunatic.'

Proby walked heavily upstairs. Rootham had begun to lift the bedroom carpet.

'Anything?'

'Not a sausage!'

He walked into the little sitting room. The presents had been unwrapped. They sat neatly on the sofa, the two shirts, the pen, the cologne, the travelling clock and the book of poetry. He opened it.

> I
> and you
> and all the weird
> vituperative ingestion of the spheres
> can hardly parse
> your pain
> enow.

Proby put it down. He walked into the bathroom. Two men were dusting for fingerprints. Would they find Sheila's? Sauntering down the corridor, he came to a narrow doorway he hadn't noticed before. Of course the house must have an attic. Climbing the steep bare stairs, he found Maggie on her hands and knees, examining the boards with a thick lens.

'Halloa Watson!' She was irrepressible. 'The room I'm going to concentrate on,' she added, 'is the room he hasn't left since we arrived. Can you get him out of there?'

'Of course.' They went downstairs together.

'Henry.'

'My dear Inspector.'

Were his nerves beginning to fray?

'I should like to have a chat with you in the kitchen.'

'Do I need my solicitor present?'

Proby looked at him thoughtfully. 'That's up to you,' he said. 'But there's no question of your being charged, and a refusal to co-operate could only place you in a rather unfavourable light.'

'Why the kitchen?'

'So they can examine this room.'

'I see.' Henry led the way through the hall and out

down the dark kitchen corridor. The kitchen itself was empty, though there were signs of a detailed search. The gas cooker was out of alignment, and two of the drawers still gaped.

'No Mrs Bertram?'

'No,' said Henry. 'I told her not to bother. Just as well! She'd have had a fit at this lot.' He smiled. 'So?'

'Let's sit down.' Proby pulled out one of the red lacquered rustic chairs. They were surprisingly comfortable. 'Tell me a bit more about Anne.'

'You knew her as well as anyone. I loved her, she loved me. She hadn't an enemy in the world.'

'What were you going to give her for Christmas?' There was a definite pause, the unmistakable frisson of a shot hitting home. Henry was carefully re-lighting his cigar stub. Why buy her a Christmas present, when she wasn't going to live that long?

'I hadn't decided,' he answered sadly, expelling a long spiral of grey smoke. 'I had thought of a dress from Rico. I'm afraid I always left it to the last minute.' He raised his eyes in mocking self-deprecation. The first lie. Proby had a clear memory of Anne telling them how perfectly chosen her presents from Henry always were. 'He spends months planning,' she had said ruefully. 'It's his job, but it makes it so tricky for poor me!'

'I see.' He paused to consider the best way forward. 'When did you open her presents to you?' Henry's eyes flickered, and rose very slowly to meet his. He'd never noticed before what long lashes they had. Was that what had attracted Sheila?

'This afternoon,' he drawled, no other word for it. He had gone into slow motion.

'And what did you do with the enamel brooch?' He could actually see Henry's mind working. It was as if he had been given stereoscopic vision into the intricate kaleidoscope of the brain's computer. Or was Henry hypnotizing him? His eyes seemed to be swelling. Was he going to shout? Demand his rights? In the end he did

114

nothing. He didn't even answer the question.

'I'm very tired,' he said. 'You'll have to forgive me. Perhaps we can continue this conversation later. I'll stay here until your men have finished, then I'm going to bed.'

Proby stood up. He had no evidence to justify an arrest, nothing beyond an absolute certainty now that this man, outwardly so respected, had slaughtered four young women for a reason that eluded explanation. It was dark outside and the wind was thundering in the chimney as he walked back across the stricken hall, its furnishings still piled pitiably against one wall.

'I'm going back to my office,' he announced to Rootham. 'Join me there when they're finished.' And he told him to start all over again, to find the brooch which he described in every detail.

Chapter 18

'Nothing?'

'Nothing.'

Proby sighed. 'No revolver, and no brooch.' He said it with a sense more of impatience than defeat. It was just a matter of time now. In the first shock of a murder investigation, those involved often tell pointless lies, hoping to conceal the meagre little skeletons that lurk in the most ordinary of cupboards. But they are easily unravelled, and just as easily understood. Henry's concealment and inexplicable lies about the Christmas presents could have no such simple explanation at this late stage. It was exactly the sort of inconsistency that pointed the way of guilt.

He was sitting at his desk opposite Rootham and Maggie. There was a knock on the door, and Julie brought in the post mortem notes on Lomi. He studied them, and passed them to Maggie.

'HIV positive?'

'Not surprising, poor kid. Anything more from the computer?'

Julie shook her head. 'I saw Hickock just now,' she said as she went out. 'He was in the lift, heading for the seventh floor.' Proby grunted. The last person he wanted to think about was Hickock.

'What next?' If Rootham was thinking of his wife and children at home, celebrating Christmas without him, he certainly wasn't showing it to Proby, or to this blonde bit from London. He was watching her covertly . . . a 36D, perhaps? And legs! He wouldn't mind . . . another knock on the door. Julie again, frowning.

'The Chief's back,' she said. 'Wants to see you in his office now.'

'He won't be happy with what I've got to tell him,' said Proby. 'Let's get it over with.' He left them there, and strode down the corridor to the lift. The building was largely deserted. Rising to the seventh floor, he walked slowly down to the imposing portal at the end and knocked.

'*Come!*' He walked in. The Chief Constable's face was a study in discontent.

'Sit there, will you?'

Proby settled himself down. The other placed his elbows on his desk and stared across.

'You've got an excellent record, Proby. You've done good work here.'

'Thank you, sir.'

'I'm taking you off this case.'

'May I ask why?'

'Oh yes, you certainly may. You may also ask why you are suspended as of now. There's no room for personal grievances in the sort of force I run, let me assure you of that!' All said with perfect patrician grace.

'And the answer?' Proby was fortunate in not really possessing a temper.

'I'll ask the questions,' snapped the other. 'Do you deny that your wife is involved with Henry Bryant?'

'No.'

'No?' It was almost a squeak.

'No. She is involved with him. That complicates the position, but in no way affects my judgement of the matter.'

'How can you possibly say that?'

'Because it's true.'

The Chief stared at him. 'Why didn't you tell me this before?'

'I only discovered myself one, two days ago. Even then I couldn't be sure. It's unfortunate.'

'Unfortunate?'

'Yes, sir.' Proby still spoke in his usual calm voice. 'It's unfortunate. But I am absolutely convinced that he is our man.'

'You used that warrant?'

'Yes, sir.'

'And found?'

'What we expected to find – nothing.'

'I've had one of your own officers in here, warning me that the *Gazette* is going to publish a story implicating you in a vendetta against Bryant. What do you say to that?'

'If you mean Hickock, I had him transferred last week for selling information to the press. If the *Gazette* prints lies, I've the same rights against libel as the man in the street.'

'Look at the time,' moaned the Chief. 'Nine o'clock on Christmas night. My wife's got ten guests for dinner, and I'm here discussing whether one of my senior detectives has to protect the name of my force by suing the local rag for libel!'

'Give me ten days,' said Proby, standing up, the better to assert his authority over the unhappy would-be host. 'I have got one promising line to follow.'

'Tell me.'

Proby explained about the missing brooch. The Chief stared at him. 'I've never heard anything less substantial in my life. What could a missing Christmas present have to do with all this?'

'That's what I'm trying to find out,' said Proby.

'Ten days!' said the Chief. 'What then?'

'Perhaps the Chief Superintendent will be back by then!'

'Or some more women will be dead!' On this note, the Chief Constable scooped up his grey cashmere overcoat and hurried away down the stairs.

Nine-tenths of all police work is routine slog. No one knows which infinitesimal piece of the jigsaw will prove of value, but everyone knows that most pieces are a waste of time. They still have to be examined, if only to be eliminated, and the test of a good police investigating officer is whether he can inspire in each of his officers the dogged persistence and continual alertness inseparable from a long search. By the following Tuesday, they knew three things. They knew that the revolver used to kill Lomi had never been recorded on any known list of weapons. This in itself was interesting, since it strongly suggested a highly unusual source. The markings of all weapons manufactured or sold within the countries covered by Interpol had since 1951 been routinely entered. Now that the old Soviet bloc countries were co-operating, there was almost a complete world-wide index of weapons in the respective filing systems now freely accessible to Proby under the 1991 concordats. They knew that Henry was aware of the surveillance devices within his house. Careful analysis of the early tapes uncovered the minute but still identifiable sounds of his search. They also knew that the matchstick by the towpath was the only possible clue left for them at any of the four scenes-of-crime. And that proved useless too, since Forensic could tell them nothing from it, except that it had been made in Sweden, like 47 per cent of all matches sold in the United Kingdom. They had of course also learnt that their prey was a resourceful man capable of deducing Lomi's location and accomplishing her murder in spite of her armed guards. This effectively ruled out a simple maniac. If Henry was their man, all his labyrinthine and bloody efforts to point suspicion elsewhere had been tragically wasted.

'You sent for me?'
'Yes, sit down will you?' Proby examined Hickock for signs of unease. They were plentiful. He was forcing himself to meet the Inspector's gaze, but his hands were clenched and there was the hint of a tic in his left eye. In short, he looked a mess.
'I'm interested.'
'Oh yes?'

119

'You told the Chief my wife was involved with Bryant.'

Hickock dropped his eyes, and said nothing.

'How did you know?'

'I was following up his alibi, wasn't I?' the fat man blustered. 'I went to the Paradise Arms, where he was supposed to have been having a drink with her. Just routine.'

'And?'

Hickock stared at him. 'You really want to know?'

'Go on.' Proby's hands were clenched, but then, so were Hickock's.

'They were there, chatting like, for fifteen, twenty minutes. Then he went to pay the bill. Reg, that's the landlord, said he had a cock-stand like that tree they put up in the square. And then she trotted out after him. She was panting for it – those were Reg's words, you understand.' He still couldn't look at the Inspector. Proby's face showed no emotion.

'And what time was this?'

Hickock took out a small blue notebook. 'Reg reckoned they arrived at 1.10, left about 1.25. They'd both gone when the cathedral bell sounded the half, because he had to remind his missus to ring the brewers.'

'So that means he must have shot his wife, what – before 12.30, to get back from the woods, change, get down to Hampton.'

Hickock stared at him again. Did the man have no feelings?

'That would fit.'

'Surely someone must have seen him?' Proby made a note. Another job for the patient seekers after truth. 'You're back on the case,' he added. 'This is useful stuff. Find where they went. But Hickock!' he said as the other was hurrying out of the office. 'Do feel free to report the evidence to me, won't you? I don't think the Chief wants to be bothered with trivia.'

Left alone, Proby laid his head on the table and closed his eyes. He could hear the clock above the filing cabinet relentlessly recording the passing seconds. Soon he must go home to Sheila. He felt unexpectedly tender towards her. Wiping away his tears, he stood up and prepared to face the elements again.

Chapter 19

The Lord Lieutenant of the county was Sir Abraham Cassel, a genial baronet of nearly sixty years who lived in a tall thin house in the middle of some scrubby parkland on the outskirts of the village of King's Bolton. He had lost his wife ten years before, and, having no children, he lived a lonely but comfortable life, devoting his considerable energies to promoting the voluntary causes of the neighbourhood. Once a year, on New Year's Eve, he would throw his house open to those in the county whom he judged to be of service to the community. They were given game pie, copious quantities of a rich red Burgundy, followed by mince pies to go with the thimblefuls of his excellent port. Vegetarians and teetotallers had a thin time of it, but for everyone else it was an invitation much sought after. By eight o'clock, his high galleried hall, hung with rather dowdy portraits and a couple of modern nudes, was almost full. Two trestle tables at the north end held the food, while at the other end, through narrow double doors, two ancient maids struggled back and forth with trays of glasses for the thirsty benefactors of Hampton.

Strategically placed near these doors, Colonel Bridgeman was debating the merits of this year's pie over its predecessors when he caught sight of the Chief Constable.

'I say, Richard!'

'Colonel.' They shook hands. 'You know my wife Caroline?'

'Ha, ha!' The Colonel shook hands with the small

granite-faced woman indicated, with every sign of pleasure. 'Very glad to see you, my dear. I'm very glad to see your husband. I hope this means we can all drive home safely without being breathalysed at our own gates!' The Chief Constable gave a thin smile. 'I met one of your chaps the other day. Chasing poachers. Tall chap with grey hair.' He paused to consider. 'Proby!'

'Indeed?' The Chief Constable had been on the receiving end of more calls from London. He was beginning to hate the name Proby. If only the man would confine his attentions to poachers.

'Have you caught your maniac yet?' As he spoke, Henry Bryant, searching for a glass of wine, joined them.

'No,' said the unhappy Chief. 'How are you, Henry?'

'Much as you would expect,' was the sour response.

'I was asking Richard if he'd caught his madman,' pursued the relentless Colonel. 'Yes please,' he added, as one of the drooping maids tried to get past with some drinks. 'We can help you with some of those, can't we, Henry?' Having lost her vital cargo, the old woman turned drearily back the way she'd come.

'Yes,' said Henry. 'That would be a great relief to us all.'

'Not least to you, old boy,' said the Colonel, squeezing his arm sympathetically. 'I was most awfully sorry.'

The Chief Constable could stand no more. 'There's Impey from the Education Department,' he said desperately. 'Will you forgive us, we must have a word.'

'I'd like to give you a ring tomorrow,' said Henry ominously. 'There are one or two things I want to talk to you about.'

'That's right!' roared the Colonel, his eyes dancing, already seeking another glass. 'Confession is good for the soul!'

Whither Henry Bryant went, thither too went his watchers. Outside the old brick manor, three unmarked police cars were deployed, and Proby, who had caught Rootham's cold, sat coughing behind the streaming windows of the furthest one, parked on the verge just beyond the park gates. The snow had begun to melt on Boxing Day and little was left now to show for all those hours of hectic blizzard, other than discoloured slush in the roads, and the occasional patch of frosted white crust, grimly surviving in the shadowed hollows out of reach of the day's pale sunbeams. Even the air smelt less pure, as if the white perfection of the snow had also stifled the last putrefactions of the year, released now to send rank little breezes of impurity eddying through the night air.

'Nothing from that effing computer?' Braithwaite beside him shook his head. His moustache had grown quite a bit over the holiday. Proby blew his nose, cursing inwardly as he placed his sopping handkerchief back in his pocket. His throat was raw, and his eyes burnt, and he wanted a drink. Rootham's figure loomed up beside them. A thin mist was beginning to curl through the scrubby trees, beautifully back-lit by the gorgeous moon. He waited while Proby laboriously wound down his window.

'Anything interesting?'

'Not a sausage!'

The two men stared gloomily at each other. Henry was giving nothing away. And why should he? He had committed his crimes, there were no reliable witnesses, no evidence against him of any kind, nothing indeed except Proby's certainty to justify the present extravagant surveillance. He had only to sit tight to survive.

'Who's looking out for this Gaffer Gaught character?'

'Oates. He says he's been away from home for a week, but that that's quite normal.'

'Where does he live?'

'In the caravan park, back of the Halcyon housing estate.'

They could hear the sound of laughter dimly echoing across the park. Sir Abraham was making his New Year speech.

'Come on,' said Proby, 'I've had enough of this charade. Let's do something useful.'

124

'Like what?'

'We'll drop in on Gaffer Gaught, see the New Year in, just in case he's come home to celebrate.'

'What'll I tell the others?'

'Tell them where we're going. If the four of them can't keep track of that bugger, they can go back on the beat!'

Their headlights cast an eerie swathe through the floating mist. It was getting thicker. Twice they passed one of the Chief's patrol cars, waiting patiently for incautious revellers. Proby had seen the figures so far: of two thousand drivers stopped, only seventy-three showed positive when breathalysed, and exactly fifty had proved prosecutable when the process was advanced to sampling their blood. In the meantime, eighteen people had died on the roads, more than half in accidents unrelated to alcohol. They passed a sign saying Cosgrove, and another saying Claxby St Anne.

'What does that prove?' he grumbled aloud. 'WATCH OUT!' Rootham swung the wheel desperately to avoid a shambling figure who had suddenly appeared a few yards ahead. The car slithered sideways, missed the man by inches and came to a stop. Braithwaite was already out of the car and had the man by his arm. Proby got out slowly, wiping his eyes.

'You want to look where you're going,' said the man. 'Driving like that in this weather!' He was very short, with bandy legs, and a dark weather-beaten complexion. He was obviously drunk. And he was carrying a single-barrelled shotgun. Braithwaite showed him his warrant card. The man peered at it blearily.

'You'll have to read it, young man. I can't see nothing in this light.'

'It says,' explained Proby, who had joined them, with a smile, 'that he is Detective Constable Braithwaite, and that he is entitled to ask for your assistance, in particular in explaining why you are walking down the middle of the road, heavily armed.'

The man chuckled. 'This ain't "armed" as you call it,' he said. 'This here's only a rook gun. Look!' He pulled a narrow cartridge from its breach. Proby took it. A .410 gauge.

'Do you have a licence?'

'Course I do!' The man shook with noisy laughter. 'Not that your lot don't try to take it away from me every time. I've got permission –' he could hardly get the word out – 'from Mr Greetham as farms in Claxby Dale. It's all legal.'

'You're Gaffer Gaught, aren't you?' What better way to see the New Year in? The man nodded, nonplussed. 'We were just coming to see you. You've been away.'

'No law against that.'

Proby's nose had begun to run, and there were shivers running through him. 'Come on,' he said. 'We'll run you home.' The man looked unexpectedly unwilling.

'I like the walk,' he said.

'Hop in.'

Still he lingered. 'I've got my bag over there.' He pointed to the undergrowth.

'Come on then,' said Braithwaite, and walked over with him. It wasn't much of a surprise to see them returning with an old army rucksack and two dead pheasants.

'Well why not?' he blustered. 'They're wild, ain't they? This land was common land till them Bridgemans enclosed it!'

'When was that?' asked Braithwaite, genuinely interested, as he put the gun in the boot.

'Seventeen forty eight!' said the old man, with a cackle. 'And I'll tell you something else, young man. There were Gaughts here a long time afore them Bridgemans showed up.' He nodded his head vigorously, and climbed into the back beside Proby. 'You've got a nasty cold there,' he said, observing Proby closely. 'Have a pull of this!' Proby took the pocket flask gratefully and swallowed something fiery.

'Thank you,' he said, trying not to catch Rootham's eye in the driver's mirror.

'Made it myself!' crowed the old reprobate triumphantly. 'Up in the old still by them old Saxon earthworks.'

Proby grinned at him, warmed by the liquor. 'It's excellent,' he said, 'but we need to ask you about the woman who was murdered in these woods before Christmas.'

'You mean Mrs Bryant?' The atmosphere in the car grew perceptibly tense.

'You knew her?'

'Course I knew her. A lovely young lady. We often stopped for a chat in the woods. She was never too busy to pass the time of day, unlike her husband. Bit of a snob, I'd say.'

'You remember the day she died?'

Gaffer narrowed his eyes. 'Let me see,' he said. He was counting off days on his fingers. 'That would be Friday the 15th?'

'Yes.'

'That's right,' said Gaffer. 'It was the day before I travelled down to visit my cousin in Nottingham. I go there every year,' he explained, 'so as we can have a go at Lord Aswarby's birds afore Christmas. It's by way of being a tradition, see? Then he comes up here and we has a go at old Kitchener!'

'Kitchener?' Proby was momentarily thrown. The little man threw himself back in his seat with glee.

'Kitchener! That Bridgeman! That's what I calls him, on account of that great big moustache. "Your country needs you." ' Proby laughed. It was a fair analogy. In the front, Rootham and Braithwaite exchanged stupefied glances.

'Look at that beggar!'

Proby turned, startled. A fox was crossing the road ahead of them. It was lean and scrawny.

'Damned old fox,' grumbled the poacher. 'That's what Clarkie ought to be after, not bothering his head about me.'

'So you were in the woods that Friday?' Proby was anxious to get back to the point.

'Course I was. I knew old Clarkie'd be feeding his birds down by the old brickyard, so I waited in the hedge, didn't I? And Mrs Bryant came and stood right next to me. She saw me, see? She was a very smart lady.'

'What happened?'

'Well, we was talking away, joking like. And then she says, "Here comes Mr Clark!" So I kept still. And he came right up, and they chatted for five minutes, then off he goes, never guessing I was ten feet away.'

'What happened then?' The policemen were agog.

'She says, "I must be off now," and that's the last I saw of her.'

'Did she say she was meeting anyone?'

He thought. 'I see what you're on about,' he said. 'No, she didn't say she was, but I reckon she might have been. The last I heard, she was walking off down the centre ride. She was singing, you know. She always sang.'

'Can you remember what she sang?'

The old man shook his head with a sad smile. 'I'm no good with music,' he said. Then, 'One line I remember, something like "You more lucky than me". That any good to you clever chaps?'

'Did you hear any shooting?' Again they listened with anxious hope.

'No,' he said. 'I don't reckon I did. Not that I'd have been surprised if I had, what with old Clarkie and Kitchener out in the wood. Them helicopters were everywhere.'

Proby turned his head to examine the man's profile. He looked entirely serious. 'Did you say Colonel Bridgeman was in the wood?'

'Oh yes,' said Gaffer. 'I saw him on my way through the rearing pen.'

'Are you quite certain?'

'Course I am. You can't miss a tash like that. And he was wearing a white raincoat. Real daft he looked, I can tell you!'

They had reached the caravan park. One trailer, very dilapidated, had lights blazing from every window.

128

'Uh-oh!' said Gaffer, with every sign of delight. 'Ezekiel's here.' As he spoke, another little round face, smudged by six days' growth of ginger stubble, appeared at the window.

'Mornin', Gaffer!' he cried. 'What ho!' This to the three policemen. 'I see you've brought the makings of a party! Where'd you find 'em? In the cemetery?' His rheumy bloodshot eyes sparkled with malice.

'We'll keep your gun,' said Proby to Gaffer, 'until we've established the position over your licence.'

'Come in! Come in!' Gaffer had really entered into the party mood now. 'I've got plenty more of my "home-made infuriator"!'

Proby might have accepted, but for the expressions on his two subordinates' faces.

'No thank you, sir,' said Rootham. 'Not on duty.'

Gaffer paused, appeared to be looking for something.

'Lost anything, sir?' inquired Braithwaite with heavy sarcasm.

'My birds,' said the old poacher reproachfully. 'I had two birds. I need them for our dinner tomorrow.'

At a nod from Proby, Braithwaite climbed angrily out of the car, opened the boot and pulled out the two pheasants, their beautiful feathers stiff from the cold and matted with dried and blackened blood. 'Here you are, sir.' He might have been handing back a driving licence.

'Thank you, young man,' said Gaffer graciously. 'Are you sure you won't come in for a noggin?'

'Yeh! You come in here!' cackled Ezekiel from the doorway. He was wearing a filthy tartan dressing-gown, bright orange woollen stockings and heavy black boots. 'Might cheer you up!' He raised a cracked glass, full of a smoky liquid which slopped over as he waved it at the young policeman. The mere thought of these two slithering through the undergrowth was enough to give any gamekeeper a headache. Braithwaite walked back to the car.

'That was a bit of luck,' remarked Proby, as they drove

home towards Hampton. Rootham nodded at him in his mirror.

'It's about time we had some luck,' he replied.

'It all evens out in the end.' Proby sneezed, and began to search his pockets for another handkerchief. 'It's just a case of being patient.' Twice on the homeward journey, they passed shivering motorists being breathalysed at the side of the road. The policemen involved looked even more glum.

'What a way to earn a living!' laughed Rootham, as he raised a hand in passing to one of the uniformed men.

Proby didn't respond. He was fast asleep.

Chapter 20

Faced with the alternative of pulling in Colonel Bridgeman or going to London to check his alibi, Proby chose the latter. Having established that Blunt's Club was closed on New Year's Day, he followed Rootham's advice and spent the day in bed, admirably nursed by Sheila. By unspoken mutual consent, they had avoided the subject of Henry since Christmas Day. She was living in a dream world, rigorously cut off from reality. Her emotional feelings for Henry had been abruptly halted in mid-development by the Christmas dramas. He hadn't telephoned, even though she longed to tell him how she felt, what little she knew, and indeed to ask how he was. But she was too scared to telephone him herself. So there she stayed, remorselessly schooling herself to play the perfect housewife, with all her hopes and desires curdling within her. It was almost a relief to have Jim home, and ill, to give a new focus to her dreary existence.

'More broth?'

It'll be gruel next, thought Proby sourly, watching his wife's supple figure etched against the sunbeams that filtered through the bedroom blind.

'No thanks.' He could hardly speak. His throat seemed blocked by some swollen boulder, raw and spiked. His head swam, and somewhere deep inside his head, a dedicated blacksmith was hard at work with a giant hammer.

'Would you like the radio up here?' He shook his head, a painful mistake. 'Or the telly?' How do you tell someone politely to shut up and go away? 'Poor darling.' Dear

God, she was going to touch his head! He closed his eyes. When he opened them again, she had gone.

It was Henry, on the telephone.

'Darling?'

'Henry!'

'Can we talk?'

'Yes! Jim's upstairs asleep.'

In the police listening van, Maggie and Reynolds were staring at each other, aghast.

'I love you.'

'Oh, Henry. I love you so much. I've wanted to feel you near me. How are you?'

Slowly, the great spools recorded their words, relaying them to the silent listeners through their baffled earphones, storing them as evidence in the public domain.

The transcript was on the Chief Constable's desk the next morning, as Proby, much restored by the prospect of work, was rattled south on the London express.

'We didn't think he knew,' said Henry, stretching out his long legs. The Chief Constable eyed Henry's cigar with misgiving. The room was gradually filling with sour wisps of smoke.

'You're saying, are you,' he repeated slowly, 'that you believe you are the subject of Detective Inspector Proby's unjustifiable suspicions because you are having an affair with his wife?'

Henry nodded. 'I know that, as one of the unfortunate husbands of this lunatic's victims, I was bound to be carefully looked at.'

The Chief nodded warily. He wasn't quite certain of his ground in agreeing to meet this man, undeniably a suspect.

'But you must know . . . at least I'm assuming you know, Richard,' he smiled at the policeman, 'that there really is no evidence against me.'

The Chief nodded vigorously.

'Now in my branch of the service . . .'

The spectre of the Home Secretary rose up against the weary Chief.

'I did know about you and Mrs Proby,' he said.

Henry raised his eyebrows. 'Of course I realize Jim has to do his job, and I bear him no grudge . . .'

'I imagine not.' The Chief Constable's sympathies lay with Proby, whatever the social standing and professional eminence of this smooth and confident interloper.

Henry played his trump card. 'I'm seeing Sir Terence tomorrow. He's up from Whitehall to inspect my establishment. I shall need to tell him what level of surveillance I'm under. I'm sure you realize there's a considerable security implication?'

The Chief Constable had spent many hours over Christmas with the Permanent Secretary's various underlings and finally, and most anxiously, with the enigmatic mandarin himself.

'I'd guess it was a full Section 53 at the moment,' continued Henry, 'judging by the way little Maggie Rowlands popped up in church the other day.' Was he being too clever? If he'd guessed that, he'd also have known that his telephone conversations were being relayed straight to the Chief. Time to go, he decided, and stood up, shaking the Chief's hand with cheerful heartiness. 'You do realize, don't you,' he said, 'that all I want is for you to catch this bastard? But it's no fun, being fingered as the local Frankenstein.'

In London, Proby had reached St Pancras station. He stared up at the vaulting turrets, with their arched eyelid-windows climbing one above the other into the near-impossible fantasy of their elevation. What extravagant fancy had led an English railway company to erect a mad Bavarian castle in a north-eastern suburb of London rather than on a craggy peak beside the Rhine?

'Blunt's Club.'

The taxi-driver stared at him. 'You what?'

'Blunt's Club. It's in St James' Street.' He'd lost the number.

'St James' Street, Hounslow, or the one up Piccadilly?'

Trust his luck to find one of London's truly helpful drivers. 'W1,' he said. 'That's Piccadilly, I think.'

The driver sniffed.

'Doubt if it's open,' he said. 'Them clubs are usually closed till Friday.'

'Just take me there.' Proby leant back, suddenly tired.

The club proved to be a tall square building at one end of the street, with bright green railings and a heavy pair of glass doors at the top of a short flight of wide steps.

'You ought to be wearing a suit if you want to go in there,' said the cabman helpfully.

'I am wearing a suit,' said Proby. The driver eyed the green cloth, admittedly rather rumpled by the journey from Hampton, and said nothing.

Pushing open the door, Proby found himself in a large hall. In one corner stood a wooden kiosk with glass panels running the whole height of the room. Crouched behind this, and ignoring him, was an elderly man in dark-green livery.

'Excuse me.' The man was studying the racing page. Reluctantly he looked up, took in Proby's appearance and turned back to the paper without comment. Proby walked right up to the kiosk.

'I'm looking for Mr Soames.' With a loud sigh, the porter folded his newspaper.

'Good morning, Detective Inspector,' he said. 'Your office rang to say you'd be in.' Proby tried a smile. The porter just looked straight through it. 'Soames is attending to a member at the minute. Would you care to sit over there?' Beside the empty grate, a single chair, upright and uninviting, stood with its back against the wall, beneath a vast painting of a man in ceremonial robes. Proby sat on it. It was as uncomfortable as it looked. Two plump young men hurried in.

'Morning, Hope! Mr Tennyson in yet?'

'Not yet, sir.' The porter beamed. 'Mr Harry's in the bar waiting for you.' Proby looked at his watch: 11.45. He must have dozed, because suddenly a man was standing over him, a tall man, with curly eyebrows and a thin bald head.

'Inspector Proby?' It was said very softly.

'Yes.' He stood up. 'Mr Soames?' The tall man shook his head, smiling gravely.

'I'm Brodie, the secretary. I thought you'd like to see Soames in my office.'

'Thank you, Mr Brodie.'

'Major,' murmured the other. 'Come this way.' They climbed an ornate staircase, its ironwork touched with cunning flecks of gold, its carpet so thick that their progress was entirely silent. Proby gradually became aware that the building was very hot, stifling even. His shirt was sticking to his back. It was also very quiet.

'Here we are.' Major Brodie's office was a modest affair, leading off the staircase behind a jib door, concealed by a great mirror that swung open to his touch. 'And here's Soames.' The barber stood up. It hardly made a difference, he was so round. His belly was really his diameter, and he projected it proudly, one finger awkwardly inserted between belt and flesh.

'I'll leave you two together,' said the Major tactfully. 'Shout if you need anything.' Proby would have killed for some coffee, but to raise his voice in this whispering building was beyond him.

'What can I do for you, sir?' The barber had a slight lisp, like a music-hall turn. He had evasive eyes, wandering around the room, not settling anywhere.

'Colonel Bridgeman's a member here?'

The man cocked his head on one side. 'We've got two,' he said.

'This one's got a moustache.' Proby almost laughed as he said it.

'Oh! Colonel Esmond!' The barber nodded. 'A wonderful old gentleman. The other Colonel is his cousin Arthur.

But he was a Gunner. He has no moustache.'

'Thank you,' said Proby. 'It's Colonel Esmond I'm interested in. I believe he was in here before Christmas?'

'I can check.' The man reached inside his black jacket. His arms were remarkably short. 'Let me see ... yes! Friday 15th. I had Mr Elwell at 10, Lord Sennowe at 10.45, and Colonel Bridgeman ... that's your Colonel Bridgeman, at 11.30. After that, I went home. A very quiet day.'

'You're sure about the day?'

'Oh yes. You can see for yourself.' The man held out his diary, inscribed with tiny neat entries. To be here by 11.30, the Colonel must have left Hampton station by no later than the 9.15 train, the one Proby himself had taken. That would have meant leaving home half an hour earlier. By the time he returned home, Anne Bryant's body had already been removed to the mortuary. Whoever Gaffer had seen stalking through the Claxby woods, it clearly had not been Colonel Bridgeman.

Chapter 21

Any of Proby's team could have checked the Colonel's story. But his next call was the real reason why he had come to London himself. In the whole case, there was but one anomaly. Everything fitted together, or had some plausible explanation, whoever the villain might be. But why should Henry, having unwrapped the Christmas presents Anne had intended for him, conceal or destroy the missing enamel brooch? And why not offer some explanation? What emotion had his expression held? Anger? Shame? There had been a glint of something unexpected in his eyes. In some ways, it was for Proby the deciding factor in his conviction that he need look no further than Henry to solve the case. He had seen the brooch for only a few seconds, but he remembered enough about it to believe he could learn more.

'The Imperial War Museum!' This time he had a driver who needed no explanations. The cab tore through the half-empty streets, careering round the Palace and through the intricate windings of Victoria.

'Here we are!' Proby was thrown forward by the vehicle's sudden halt. 'Looks like a friend of yours.' And there indeed was a familiar monkey's face, beaming as always through the years that separated them from their early schooldays.

'Bill!'

'Jim!' Bill Adams had lived in Goonby, three streets away from the Proby household, a scrawny little boy whose father had died in a mining accident. Old Mrs

137

Adams, a formidable woman of colossal girth, had continued to provide for her family by starting up a removals business. It hadn't been a great success, but it had paid enough to send Bill to Cambridge when he failed the scholarship. And here he was, a professor no less, with a wife, several children and the OBE! If only his mother could have lived to see it.

'What's your problem this time?' It was a shared joke that Proby only got in touch when he needed help. One day, he thought, it may be the other way round. 'But first, some coffee. I can see you need it.' They took a slow lift to Bill's office. While he busied himself with cups and kettles, Proby commandeered a sheet of plain paper and began painstakingly to draw the missing brooch.

'Crikey!' His friend peered over his shoulder. 'This isn't the Natural History Museum!'

'No, look,' said Proby, 'it had a whorl like that, and these flowers.'

'I see.' The other man took down an index, and began to leaf through it. 'Like this?'

'That's it!' It certainly looked identical. 'What is it?'

'Not particularly rare. The insignia of the Royal Nassau Fencibles. Rather a chi-chi regiment, raised by George II, or rather by his friend General Lumby, to fight in the Hesse-Hanover squabble. It never came to a fight actually, because old Friedrich-Kaspar died before they could set sail, and his son wasn't interested. They made lots of these brooches. We've got one downstairs.'

'May I see it?'

They travelled back in the same slow lift.

'Is this it?'

'I'm sure it is. What's its value?'

'A couple of hundred, perhaps. A bit more if you had an ancestor in the regiment, perhaps.'

'Where would you buy one?' The professor thought.

'One of the specialist dealers. There are quite a few about. Spinks. Freddie Owen.'

'Do you have a list?' Up they crawled. Did the manu-

138

facturers of lifts know no sense of urgency?

There were two local dealers listed, one in Hampton itself. Having asked to borrow the brooch, Proby took the stairs and walked out into the street to find a taxi, to begin his journey home.

When his train drew into Hampton, the light had already faded, leaving the familiar buildings as dim silhouettes already acquiring their accustomed evening blur of drifting mist. Rootham was waiting on the platform, and they drove straight to the town address. The little shop was closed, and the rooms above it were clearly empty. Wherever the jeweller lived, it was not here. His normal hours were ten till four, with an hour off for lunch at one.

'See if you can find his name and trace him through British Telecom,' Proby told Julie over the telephone, as Rootham steered him north towards the other address, an arcade in Castlewick. This shop was lit, although it was more of a home than a shop, having no window for wares, only a plate by the door:

J. A. Templeton M.A.
Dealer in Curios
Please ring the bell

Proby turned down his collar. Miraculously, his cold had gone. He pressed the bell. He could hear nothing. He pressed it again. There were footsteps. A grumbling voice. The sound of bolts being drawn.

'Who's there?' A high-pitched querulous voice.

'Police.' The door opened a crack. He could see the chain was attached.

'Let me see your card.' He thrust his warrant card through the crack, half expecting the door to be slammed on to his wrist.

'All right.' He withdrew his hand, the door closed, and re-opened to reveal an old woman, her skin so pale as to seem almost transparent. 'What do you want?'

'I was hoping to see Mr Templeton.'

She glowered at him. 'There's no Mr Templeton here.'

'But the plate . . .'

She was practically snarling.

'You must be Miss Templeton?' It was Rootham who saved the day. Having parked behind the pub, he had come up behind Proby. She nodded.

'The Inspector and I need to ask you some questions.' He almost pushed Proby into the doorway, so that the old crone had to retreat, still arching her back like an angry cat. The house smelt of old age, and the windows had cobwebs that glinted yellow in the glow of the street lamp outside. They were full of flies. The only ornament was a stuffed cat in a broken glass case.

'Do you know what this is?' Proby laid the Museum brooch on the dingy cloth that covered her parlour table.

She stared at Rootham.

'Well, do you?' the sergeant asked. Clearly Proby was going to have to take a back seat in this interview.

She nodded. 'It's another of those Nassau Fencible brooches,' she said. 'Heaven knows why they're so popular this year.'

'Do you have one in stock?'

She actually laughed. 'I'm not Harrods, you know. I buy and sell on commission.'

'When did you last see one?'

'Six months ago.'

'Can you tell us more?' She was ignoring Proby completely.

'I'd had it, oh, five, six years maybe. And suddenly two people wanted it. Last April. Or was it May? I had Luke Lester in here on the Monday. He took it away on sale or return. The next day I had this girl in.'

'Blonde, thirtyish?' Proby couldn't stop himself.

Her face froze. She fixed her eyes on the floor.

Rootham waited a minute, then said, 'Tell us about her.'

'Young woman. Married.'

'How could you tell?'

140

'Because she was wearing a wedding ring of course.'
She eyed him with contempt.

'Did she give her name?'

A pause. 'I don't think so.'

'Can you describe her?'

'Fair hair. Middle height. Slim. A happy creature.' It
was said with envy, not with ill-will.

'Why did she want one of these brooches?' Rootham
hadn't quite got the hang of the name yet.

'For a friend of hers. Or maybe her husband. There
was some connection with the regiment, I think.'

'Did Luke Lester,' he had written the name in his notebook, 'buy the brooch?'

'Oh yes,' she said grimly. 'I expect he sold it to her
himself. I'm afraid Mr Lester is not entirely what you
might call honest.'

'Where does he operate?' But the two policemen had
already guessed the answer.

'Forty-four Market Place, Hampton. The shop is called
Its and Bits.' The address they'd just come from.

'What I don't see,' grumbled Proby as they drove back
towards Hampton, 'is how it matters. Let's assume Anne
Bryant bought the brooch from Lester. Let's further
assume that Bryant is connected with this silly regiment.
In fact,' he paused, struck by a thought, 'his initials are
H.L.B., so let's take a great leap into the unknown and
say his middle name is Lumby. That's the name of the lad
who started the regiment,' he added, catching sight of
Rootham's mystified face. 'But then what? Why should
he want to murder her for that? Or for anything? Or all
those other poor people?'

'What if it's not him at all?' Rootham kept his eyes
firmly on the road.

Proby nodded. 'I could be wrong,' he conceded. 'But
I'm not.'

141

Chapter 22

Detective Chief Superintendent Rankin was not the man to do a job which another could do as well. Stretched out on the sofa in his office, a Turkish cigarette drooping from his lips, he directed an affectionate smile at Proby.

'You've got Grace Kelly in a truly awful state upstairs,' he said, referring to their fastidious Chief. 'She's positively expiring under the pressure from Tothill Street.'

'Do you think I'm wrong about Bryant?'

The senior officer screwed his eyes into little flecks of light surrounded by wrinkles. 'No,' he said, taking the oval cigarette between two fingers and blowing a thin fountain of smoke towards Proby. 'I think you're right. The Chief gave you ten days from Christmas. You've got two left. If you can't do something very quickly, I reckon you're going to be volunteered to head the new traffic division.'

'You can't be serious.'

The Superintendent giggled. 'Chief Inspector pays better than what you get now. Grace has stuck up for you pretty well. But *they* want you off the case.'

'Who's "they"?'

The older man shrugged. 'Politicians. Civil servants. From the sound of it, they care more about their pet Henry Bryant than they do about a few young women in the provinces.'

'You're joking!'

'Of course. But you aren't popular. It's the Sheila business that leaves a nasty taste in the mouth.'

Proby stared at him. 'And in mine!' he protested.

The Superintendent raised a languid hand. 'Two days, Jim. Make something stick!'

At ten o'clock the next morning Proby and Rootham were sitting smoking in their car outside a butcher's shop, across the street from Its and Bits. It had a large window and you could see right into the shop. Only there was no one there.

'Bastard!' Rootham had started the day badly. A row with Mollie over who cooked breakfast had been followed by his elder twin daughter's admission that her maths teacher had been fondling her. Now Luke Lester was late. He wanted to hit something, or someone. After careful thought, he decided it should definitely be someone.

'Here he is.' Down the street, a lithe young man swinging a handbag was hurrying with an air of purpose. 'Just what you'd expect.' He walked straight past. A woman coming the other way crossed the road just in front of them, pausing to return their stare. It was 10.15. They could just hear the cathedral clock. Someone tapped on Proby's window.

'You can't park here.' The warden had a pimple, right on the tip of his nose.

'Clear off!' said Rootham savagely, and thrust his warrant card into the man's offended face.

'Only doing my . . .' They could hear his wounded voice whining its way up the street. 'Some folks got no . . .' Rootham wanted to get out of the car and go after him, stave in his fucking ribs!

Proby laid a cautionary hand on his friend's arm. 'Come on then,' he said. 'What's eating you?'

Rootham told him. 'She's only eleven! Can't anyone keep their innocence in this effing sewer? He won't remember enough to teach the effing alphabet when I've finished with him!'

Privately, Proby guessed he'd feel the same way himself if he had children. As it was, he was able to preach

143

common sense. They were still arguing about it when a pale chubby man, wrapped in heavy coat and scarf, let himself into the shop, peering awkwardly through thick spectacles at the three locks with which his door was protected.

'Here we go!' The two men jumped out of the car. The little man took one look at them and dashed into his shop, ramming home all the inside bolts as soon as he was inside. For a moment Proby thought he might be going to stick his tongue out at them. He reached inside his coat, and saw the little man's eyes open wide with terror. He smiled. It didn't seem to help. He pressed his identification against the glass. The jeweller peered at it, screwing up his eyes in a parody of short-sightedness.

'Shall I just smash the door down?' Rootham was itching to have a go.

'Keep calm!' The man was opening up.

'Inspector Proby?' Apparently he could read after all. 'I've been expecting you.'

'You mean . . .?'

'Mrs Bryant. She came in here last summer. I've been meaning to ring you.'

'Because . . .?'

'Because she had a friend with her. A man friend.'

An hour later, they were still going over the same ground. He'd spotted Anne's photograph in the paper only two days ago. She'd come in with this man. Forties, thin, athletic looking. About six foot. Light brown hair, cleft in chin. The man had bought Anne the enamel, having spoken a couple of times on the telephone to Lester in preceding weeks. It was pure luck that Lester had remembered that old Pussy Templeton had one. He'd paid her two hundred and forty pounds, and got six hundred from the man, paid in cash. Twelve fifty-pound notes. No, he'd forgotten to enter the transaction in his cash book. He was disgracefully behind with it. But he didn't have to get it up to date until 5 April. Yes, of course it would all be declared to the Inland Revenue. His eyes twinkled at Proby through the thick lenses. 'Believe that, and you'll believe anything,' he seemed to be saying.

'And you can't remember his name?'

'No! I wish I could.'

'How did she address him?'

'I've told you . . . "darling" or "dearest".'

'And it definitely wasn't this man?'

The jeweller stared hopelessly at the photograph of Henry for the tenth time. 'No,' he said. 'It wasn't him. That's her husband, isn't it? That's Rupert.'

'Who's Rupert?'

'Isn't he called Rupert?'

'No,' said Proby very quietly. 'So who's Rupert?'

'Did I say Rupert?'

Rootham's hand had curled into a fist.

'Yes,' said Proby.

'Oh well,' said the little man, 'I expect this other man was called Rupert. Certainly one of them was.'

'Take him back to the station. Get the whole thing down on paper.' Proby stood up. 'I'm going up to see him.'

'On your own?'

There was no reply.

Proby took a taxi straight to Claxby. As he expected, Henry was sitting smoking in his study. He must be under colossal strain.

'You're back.'

'Who's Rupert?'

'Rupert?'

'A friend of Anne's.'

'Why do you ask?'

'Because he's a new suspect.'

Henry eyed him thoughtfully. 'I've put in a complaint about you.'

Proby grinned. 'There aren't many who don't,' he said. 'So who's Rupert?'

'You think he might be involved?'

'Yes. It's possible.'

'You think I did it.' It was a challenge.

'That's possible too. I have to keep my options open.'

'Rupert Beddoes was a casual acquaintance of Anne's.' It was said dismissively. 'But it can't have been him.'

'Why not?'

'He killed himself last June. Jumped under a tube in London. Quite unexpected. Anne was very sad at the time.' He was laughing. Under that cool temperate exterior, Proby could make out a man positively hugging himself with glee.

'Oh well,' he said. 'Another blind alley. Thanks for the information.'

'Mind how you go!' The two men looked at each other. Henry was in the process of lighting another cigar, and his gaze travelling down its length seemed to be assessing Proby as a gunner might scan his target through the sights of a cannon. Proby stood up. As the other made no move, but stayed there scrutinizing him with that same unnerving air of calculation, he made himself walk to the door, through the musty hall and out of the building. In passing through the porch, he felt again the muted warmth of the morning sun filtered through the heraldic glass, bathing him in a scarlet sacrificial light.

Chapter 23

'I'm sorry, Jim.' Chief Superintendent Rankin smoked only Turkish cigarettes, little oval cylinders that left a rich sultry aroma on the air. 'But I think you'll understand why the Chief has to move you on.'

'Because he's my wife's lover as well as our murderer?'

'Yes.'

'So at least you agree with me?'

The Chief Superintendent shrugged his heavy shoulders with languorous exaggeration. 'You're not often wrong, Jim. Who am I to say? But one thing I do know, you're off the case!' He laughed. 'Take some holiday. Leave me to struggle in the pond for a bit. If I were you . . .'

Proby glowered at him. 'Well?'

'I'd explore London. Get to know the secret little places.'

'Why?' Proby was tired of his superior's manner.

'Because,' said the older man, suddenly hardening his expression, 'it's not all that easy to tip a man under a tube train without anyone seeing.' They stared at each other.

'You'd recommend a fortnight's leave in London?' said Proby after a pause.

'I would.' The senior officer smiled. 'You never know your luck.'

'This is an unexpected pleasure, Jim.' Bill Adams lived in Swinton Street, at the back of King's Cross, in a grubby little Victorian house that had altogether escaped the cold hand of modernization. A bed of scarlet coals shifted

147

angrily in the grate, sending out reassuring orange flares of heat, and the heavy brown velveteen curtains hid the wintry scene outside. The wallpaper must once have shown a colourful riot of rambling roses, but time, the fire and Bill's pipe had reduced it to a faded sepia wash of inert half-tones, smudged here and there by the long-departed Adams children. The fireside chairs even had embroidered antimacassars.

Proby smiled. 'The treat is mine,' he said. 'You know what you've done?' His friend shook his head, puzzled. 'You've re-created Goonby in central London. If I half-close my eyes, this could be your mother's house, or mine. It's lovely. In fact,' the picture above the chimneypiece had suddenly caught his eye, 'that is surely, yes, that is the same picture of Goondale your mother had!'

Bill grinned. 'It certainly is. We all got our pick. That was my choice. Those were happy days.' The two friends sat smoking in contented silence. Cath Adams, a fierce woman with dark watchful eyes, had brought them each a pint mug of ale. Now she was leaving them be, busy with her own mysterious rituals in the basement. From time to time they could hear unexplained sounds, a crash, some weird singing and then, even more disturbing, a loud laugh. But then, as they chatted about the past, a magnificent smell crept up the stone stairwell, seeping under the old pine door – the unmistakable scent of seething oxtail.

'Cath was thrilled to get your call.'

'You're sure this isn't an imposition?' Proby was rather afraid of his friend's strange wife. She had sounded far from enthusiastic at his tentative enquiry about a bed for a few days. He hadn't liked not to ask, so pressing had been Bill's invitations over the years. But having asked, he had even been intimidated by her stern confirmation. Of course he would pay them something before he left, but he half expected she would throw it back in his face.

'No, no.' Bill laughed at Proby's expression. 'That's just her way. You never met my in-laws? They were gypsies,

148

the real thing. Cath was brought up in a proper painted horse-drawn caravan, not one of these gin palaces you see nowadays. You know what my father-in-law said when I told him I wanted to marry his daughter?' Proby shook his head politely. 'He said, "You can send her home any time. But cheat on her while she's with you, and I'll cut your rocks off myself." How's that for making a fellow feel at home!' He roared with laughter. 'She'd never been to school at all. But I reckon she knows a sight more than most of my colleagues at the Museum.' The door opened and the redoubtable Cath gave him a silent nod. 'Come on then,' he cried. 'Tea's on the table! We'll be in trouble if we don't do it justice.'

They sat opposite each other as the silent woman served them the oxtail, with thick slices of buttered bread and strong sweet tea. She was still beautiful, though it was impossible to guess her age. He knew she had borne and raised six children, yet her figure was as slim and svelte as a teenager. Her cheekbones glinted in the half-light and her wide unpainted mouth never changed from its humourless set. Whatever had made her laugh, it wasn't going to be repeated in front of Proby.

The next morning he took the tube to South Kensington, and walked down Sloane Avenue to the local police station. Forewarned, they had already laid out the case-notes on Rupert Beddoes' death, together with a newly typed list of the witnesses and next of kin, the pathologist's report and his telephone number. There were two main witnesses, a typist and a stockbroker, and only one family member listed, Miss Rachel Beddoes, who had given her address as Flat 7, 124 Chelsea Grove Mansions. She had described herself as an actress. Beddoes had been unlucky. The train had missed his head, ripped off both legs and then entangled him within its undercarriage. It had taken them forty minutes to reach him, and several people on the platform had had to be treated for shock. He had died just as the doctor was giving him the merciful morphine.

149

Grim-faced, Proby took copies of the statements, and then returned to the interview room he'd been allocated by the helpful desk-sergeant to make some appointments. Neither the typist nor the stockbroker were in. He left messages on their ansaphones, giving Bill's number, and dialled Miss Beddoes.

'Yes?'

'Miss Rachel Beddoes?'

'Who's that?' She sounded breathless, hopeful.

'Detective Inspector Proby. It's about your brother.'

'Oh.' She couldn't disguise her disappointment. 'My brother?'

'Rupert Beddoes.'

'What about him?' Her voice was cold, impatient.

'I'd like to come and see you if I may.'

'What – now?' It was most discouraging.

'Please.'

'All right,' she said reluctantly. 'But please get off the line. I'm expecting a very important call.' Obediently, he replaced his receiver without another word.

Chelsea Grove Mansions was less than ten minutes' tramp through the slushy streets from the police station. Eight storeys high, it dominated the surrounding roads of pretty lime-washed cottages with its massive red-brick majesty, but a majesty tarnished by years of imperfect maintenance. Long black stains down the brickwork spoke of blocked gutters, wrinkled window-frames illustrated the pointless task of painting rotten timber, and the impressive variety of locks on the unattended main door suggested a futile battle against casual crime. A hand-written notice by the door read, 'The video-lock is out of order. Please ring the appropriate bell long and loudly.' To the left of the door was a rusty panel divided into sections with each bell having a slot for a card beside them, all empty. Checking his list, Proby rang number 7. Nothing happened. He glanced at his watch. Half past eleven. He rang again.

'I can hear you. Just wait, will you. I'm on the telephone.' A window slammed shut above him. He knotted his scarf tighter round his neck, stamped his feet, and waited. Presently a short woman in something white appeared on the other side of the door, and began to open the locks.

'Come in quickly,' she said. 'You're letting the cold in.' She was wearing a night-dress. 'You'd better come up.' They were half-way up the stairs when she paused. 'I suppose you do have some identification?' He smiled and produced his warrant card, which she waved away impatiently. 'We're always being told to check. Ten of these flats were done over last month alone.'

Her flat was surprisingly neat. There was a little hall with a flimsy gilt table piled with magazines, a doorway off leading into a shiny white kitchen, and another which she led him through into a large room with three tall windows. It was impossible to ignore the bed in the corner, half covered by a brilliantly patterned patchwork quilt. Perhaps she had been tidying it while he waited outside.

'I expect you want some tea?'

He was half-frozen. To have refused would have been an act of madness. 'Yes please,' he said.

As expected, she pulled a face, and disappeared into the kitchen. Her night-dress hid nothing, heavy breasts, full stomach, sagging bottom. Was this how she received all her visitors? He walked over to the desk. There were two photographs, both of herself.

'Make yourself at home,' she said. She was carrying two mugs. 'With milk or without? I don't keep sugar.'

'With, please.'

She handed him one of the mugs. 'It's Lapsang Souchong.'

'Thank you,' he said. It could have come from Timbuctoo for all he cared. 'Do you have a picture of your brother?' She shook her head. 'None at all?' He was amazed. The report said they were twins.

'I threw them out,' she said curtly. 'No good maunder-

151

ing on about the past. On to the next thing, I say.'

'Were you surprised that he should kill himself?'

She glared at him. 'Of course he didn't kill himself,' she snapped. 'He had everything to live for. He was the very last person to think of suicide.'

'What makes you so sure?'

'We were twins, you know.'

'Yes.'

'Our parents brought us up very strictly. He would never have abdicated responsibility like that.'

'Responsibility to whom?' Her age was given as thirty-one, but if he'd had to guess he'd have put it nearer forty.

'To life,' she said robustly. 'To his friends.'

'To you?'

She shook her head with a slight smile. 'I didn't need his brand of self-righteousness. But I do know the coroner got it round his neck.'

'Who were his close friends?'

She paused to take stock. 'Half a dozen mates from the army. Couple of blokes from school. Girlfriends. Why?'

'Anne Bryant?'

She snorted with disgust. 'That dreadful woman. So stuck-up and pompous. I couldn't bear her. They used to go on namby-pamby expeditions together buying old clothes for their pet charities. She certainly wasn't a girl-friend. She was married to some equally frightful man in the Midlands. Why do you mention her?'

'She was murdered just before Christmas.'

She stared at him. 'You mean that maniac up in Hampton? I read about that. What's that got to do with Rupert?'

'I was hoping you'd tell me.'

'Do you want to sit down?' He perched himself on a rickety metal chair. Anything to keep away from that bed. Sure enough she settled herself back on it, with no pretence at modesty. 'Tell me who you are again.'

'Proby,' he said cautiously. 'I'm just down here on holi-day, and I thought I'd follow up the details of some of

152

those connected. Your brother's name came up as a friend of Mrs Bryant's.'

'I see,' she said. 'Are you married?'

'I am,' he said, forcing a smile. 'We're going to a musical tonight.'

'Well, I hope you both enjoy it,' she said. 'My God! Here's my telephone call. See yourself out if that's all.' She snatched up the receiver. 'Yes! Who is it?'

Proby took his cup into the kitchen, but left it hurriedly on the draining board when he heard her conversation tailing off. Back in the fresh air, he picked up a passing cab, and settled down to make some notes during the long crawl back to Swinton Street.

Chapter 24

'Tell me about your wife. She's called Sheila, isn't she?' Bill Adams was out late lecturing on the Crimean War to a post-graduate group from London University. As a result, Proby found himself back beside the fire, but with his hostess opposite him curled up in the old leather wing chair.

He smiled at her. 'Yes.'

'Adams says she is very beautiful, and much younger than you.' He couldn't quite get used to her impersonal habit of addressing her husband in this way. Nor could he recall Bill having ever met Sheila. 'Has that been a problem?'

'I don't think so,' he said stiffly. To his consternation, she burst out laughing. 'Why . . .?'

'Oh, you mustn't be cross with me for laughing,' she said. She was even wiping her eyes. 'It's just that you are so like Adams. Anyone could tell you come from the same village, the same street even!'

Mollified, he smiled back. 'I'm sure that's true.' She looked quite different when she unbent, the harsh contours of her face softening into a dangerously animal sensuality. No wonder Bill had braved his mother's fury in ignoring the Goonby girls in favour of this mysterious woman.

'So why are you so unhappy?'

His face froze again. 'I don't think I said I was.'

She shook her head. 'There's no need,' she said. 'Your whole manner shouts it from the rooftops.'

'I imagine every marriage has its tricky moments.'

She nodded. 'Has she had many lovers?' He made to stand up, but something about her held him in his place. 'It is easier to talk to a stranger. And you and I will always be strangers.'

'I hope not,' he heard himself saying, in a depressingly pompous tone.

'Oh yes,' she said. 'Because while I would have you take me on the floor this moment, you would never betray Adams.' He stared at her, his mind churning between sudden desire and baffled embarrassment. 'You see?' she said. 'We will always be strangers. There can be no accord between the man and the woman, until they have tasted each other.' She stood up with a curious smile. 'I see that you want me, but you will not dare. So I cannot help you with your marriage.' After she left, he stayed staring sightlessly into the dying coals until Bill returned from his lecture.

'Has Cath looked after you all right?' he said cheerily, angling the coal-scuttle so that a generous heap of fresh coal tumbled on to the grey embers.

'She certainly has,' replied his friend. 'We had hotpot with dumplings. What a cook!'

'You must come more often,' said Bill. 'She likes you.'

The next morning came calls both from Tracy Brown the typist and Adrian Drage the stockbroker He was to meet the former after work at her digs in Walthamstow, while the latter volunteered to meet him at a café off the Bayswater Road around eleven.

'I'll drive you there,' offered Bill. 'I don't have to be in Lambeth until lunchtime.' His wife, having served them breakfast, had retreated again to the basement. She had reverted to her previous silence. Proby couldn't help noticing that his friend had two very prominent love-bites on the side of his neck.

The Bimbashi Café was a gloomy affair, stinking of sour spices and even a hint of vomit. Very gingerly, Proby settled himself at the table nearest to the door and ordered a bottle of mineral water.

155

'Very fine coffee?' He shook his head, and opened the newspaper he had bought on his way down Queensgate.

'Are you Proby?' He looked up to find a plump young man in a loud pinstriped suit standing staring at him with his hands on his hips. He nodded. 'Thought so. You look exactly like a policeman from Hampton.'

'Thank you!' They both laughed.

'Sorry to choose such a hole. I was made redundant last year, and this is the cheapest place hereabouts.'

'In that case,' said Proby sympathetically, 'let me buy you a cup of coffee.'

'You must be joking!' cried the young man. 'I can't risk caffeine these days. Hi! You! A large sweet lassi and a big bowl of almond kulfi since my friend here is paying. Sure you won't join me?' Proby shook his head. Even his water smelt strange. 'Bloody cold, isn't it?' He sat down. 'So?'

'You were present when Rupert Beddoes fell under a District Line train last summer.'

'I certainly was. Never heard such screaming. And it went on for hours. I thought it was supposed to be a quick way of going. Dreadful.' He shook his head violently at the memory. 'One young woman fainted, you know.'

'You were standing beside him when he fell?'

'Well, I didn't push him if that's what you mean. Thank you,' he added to the waiter who had brought him a tall glass with a milky mixture. 'Don't forget my kulfi.'

'No, I'm not suggesting you did. But could someone else have?'

The young man put down his drink. His mouth was stained with a thick white residue. 'What's all this about?'

'Just a routine check. Could someone else have pushed him?'

'There were a lot of people there. Most of them stayed at first, but when that screaming kept on and on, a lot left. There were quite a few crying. I mean, men as well as women.'

'Do you recognize this man?' Proby took out a photo-

156

graph of Henry Bryant and passed it over the table.

The young man stared at it, then wiped his mouth. 'Who's this?'

'Have you ever seen him before?' Proby could almost taste the excitement within himself.

'No.' The other handed the picture back. 'Never clapped eyes on him. You reckon he did it?'

'He wasn't among the crowd?'

'I'm telling you, the face means nothing to me.'

Proby placed a five-pound note on the table. 'I hope this will cover the bill,' he said. 'Thank you for helping.' The stench of the place was making him ill.

He lunched quietly in a McDonald's in Oxford Street, then spent an hour window-shopping before catching a Central Line train to Oxford Circus and changing to the Victoria Line for Walthamstow. At both stations, he waited for two or three trains to pass before boarding. Sometimes he stood directly behind an imaginary victim, sometimes alongside. There seemed only one way to propel a man under a train without being obvious about it. And given that Beddoes had died in June, perhaps it might have made his murderer conspicuous in a different way. At Walthamstow he commandeered the station-master's telephone and rang the pathologist who had dealt with Beddoes. By good luck, he was in.

'Have you still got your report on the body?'

'Somewhere. What is it you want, Inspector?'

'I want to know if there was a wound or a contusion caused before death at the base of his spine?'

'Is that all? Have you any idea what shape that torso was in when it got to me?' He sounded outraged.

'This may turn out to be a murder inquiry. I'm sorry to be a nuisance.'

'No,' the other man sounded more tired than angry, 'I'll go and check. Which department did you say you were from?'

Proby, who was acting without authority and in the Met's province, decided not to reply.

'Like that, is it?' muttered the pathologist. 'Some of you chaps spend more time checking up on each other than you do on solving crime. I'll go and have a look.' Proby waited patiently for nearly five minutes, warding off the increasingly frustrated station-master with a selection of anxious smiles. 'Yes,' said a voice suddenly in his ear as he was beginning to doze. 'There was time for quite a bruise to develop. The photographs are not clear, because of all the other damage. It's just above the base of the spine. I'd assumed it was yet another piece of train hitting the poor blighter. Are you saying it was something else?'

'Could it have been caused by the tip of an umbrella?'

A pause. 'Yes. Yes it could.'

'Thank you, Doctor.' Proby hung up. Turning left out of the station, as the girl had explained, he headed up the road until he found Gidea Park Lane on his right. Tracy's address was number 75, a small privately run hostel. She was looking out for him, and led him up two flights of stairs into a glaring red room, hung with Afghan rugs.

'This is Luther,' she said. A young man with long dreadlocks stood up politely and took Proby's hand. 'We're just finishing our tea. Would you like something?' It smelt delicious, but he shook his head. In two hours' time, he'd be facing another of Cath's colossal concoctions. 'It's about that dreadful accident, isn't it?'

He nodded. 'I want to ask you to think back. You were beside him when he fell?'

'Yes,' she said. 'It was so awful. He screamed and screamed, like a pig.'

'Did you actually see him jump?'

She screwed her eyes up. Her hair was intricately plaited and had a bluish sheen over its dense blackness. Luther watched her with large patient eyes. It was obvious that they were in love, just from the way that their bodies echoed each other's movements. 'No,' she said at last. 'He seemed so normal. I'd dropped my shoulderbag, and he'd picked it up for me, with such a nice smile. I turned to

158

watch the train coming in, and then several people cried out. That was when the screaming started. They kept moving the train, you see. To get him out. But he was caught in the machinery, or so they said in court.'

'Does this man look familiar?' Proby passed her the picture of Henry Bryant. She stared at it. 'Could he have been at the station?'

'At the same time, you mean?'

'Yes.'

She stared again, then showed the picture to Luther.

'Well, it's no good asking me,' he said, smiling. 'I wasn't there!'

She handed it back, shaking her head. 'Sorry,' she said. 'Never seen that one.'

'What was the weather like that day?' said Proby, following his earlier train of thought.

She thought again.

'I can tell you that,' said Luther, delighted to be able to contribute at last. 'It was boiling hot. I was selling ties in the Camden market. I'd sold two of Rangin's, but when I came home to celebrate, you were hollering about this guy under the train!'

She nodded. 'That's right. It was very hot.'

'This man,' said Proby, 'was carrying an umbrella.'

She stared at him.

'Do you remember him now?'

She took back the photograph. 'No,' she said. 'But I do remember someone with an umbrella. It had a funny handle, I remember thinking it looked a bit like sugar-cane, only yellow.'

Chapter 25

Rootham rang the next morning to say the surveillance on Henry Bryant had been lifted, and that Sheila had left a message with him to say she had gone to stay with her parents in Harrogate.

'How's the investigation?' Proby couldn't resist asking.

'Gone to pieces!' was the gratifying reply. 'Morale rock bottom, Super demanding more fancy computer support, Chief spouting about commitment; nothing changes! When are you coming back?'

'Sooner than I thought. I've got one more person to talk to. I might be able to catch the late train tonight.'

'Want to be met?'

'You must be joking! I'm on holiday, remember?'

'You came back.'

He nodded. She was wearing a shabby blue housecoat, hardly less revealing than her negligee, and the bed had clearly seen some action in his absence. The patchwork quilt was screwed up in a ball in the corner, and there were two glasses on the bedside table. She caught his glance and smiled. 'I may be getting the role of Gertrude in a new production of *Hamlet*,' she said.

'Is that good?'

She stared at him. 'Yes,' she said, 'it's a wonderful part.'

He sat down on the metal chair. 'I've got a part for you too,' he said. 'But I'd better warn you. It could be dangerous.' She stared at him, her mouth slightly open, her shoulders hunched. What on earth could she see in a middle-aged not to say old policeman, his hair grey, his

160

mind wholly taken up with the cruelties and perversions of criminal activities? 'Are you very lonely?' he couldn't help asking.

She shrugged. 'It goes with the job. So what do you want me to do?'

He explained, and as he did so, her face grew tense and thoughtful. By the time he had left, her eyes held the vacant look that for her characterized the preparation necessary to portray a new impersonation.

'I'm sorry you're leaving so soon.' Bill was in his bedroom, watching him pack. 'I'll walk with you to the station. It's only just across the road.'

'I've had a fascinating time,' said Proby, sincerely.

'So you will come again?'

'Of course.'

'Cath was afraid she'd put you off.' Proby looked up from his suitcase. His friend met his gaze without embarrassment. 'She's a very individual person,' Bill went on. 'I love and respect her more than I could explain to anyone. But I've never tried to impose my values on her, any more than she has imposed hers on me.'

'She's a great cook!' They grinned at each other.

'So you'll be back?'

'Yes, please.'

'Soon?'

'As soon as I can.' They walked downstairs. Cath was standing beside the front door. Proby put down his suitcase to shake her hand, and Bill picked it up and carried it down the steps into the road.

'Goodbye,' he said, 'and thank you.'

'Goodbye,' she said. 'I'm sorry I couldn't help you with your wife.' He smiled politely, and followed Bill down the steps. 'Because you see,' she murmured after him, 'you may not have much time left.' He halted and turned round, looking up into her strange dark eyes. 'Don't miss your train,' she said, and turned back into the house.

*

161

As Proby's train rattled over the icy points through the dark snow-covered fens, Henry tried dialling Sheila for the tenth time that day. The number rang without response. He knew that Proby was away and that he was no longer under suspicion, but where was Sheila? No sooner had he put the phone down than it began to ring.

'Yes?'

'Mr Bryant?' A woman's voice.

'Who's that?'

'You won't remember me, but we were standing next to each other on South Kensington station last summer.'

'I'm afraid . . .'

'I saw your picture in the papers, you see. I didn't know who you were before.'

'How did you get my number?' His mind was rapidly calculating the different ways of dealing with the call.

'I'm afraid I was rather naughty. Once I discovered you were ex-directory, I got it from your village shop.'

'That was clever of you.' He could almost see her self-satisfaction.

'I felt sure you'd help. I couldn't forget that umbrella with its yellow handle!'

'Help?' He'd had to bite his lip to keep calm.

'Yes. Knowing you from that time on the station, something told me you'd want to help with my mortgage. They're threatening to repossess my little flat.'

'Are you trying to blackmail me, Miss . . .?'

'Mrs Brown. No, of course not.'

'I think this conversation should continue at a police station.'

'Certainly,' she said, her voice hardening. 'If that's what you'd prefer. I would have given evidence at that poor man's inquest. Only there didn't seem any point. You'd disappeared, and I didn't want any bother. But now that I've found you . . . I'm sorry about your wife, but it's an ill wind!' She actually chuckled. 'It was funny, that umbrella. Until I saw why you'd brought it out on a sunny day. Ooh, I've got to go now. I'll ring you tomorrow.' The line went dead. The worst part was how calm she sounded, how certain that he would co-operate. Slowly, he crossed to his chair by the fire, took out a cigar and settled down to think.

Chapter 26

Proby, meanwhile, was enjoying Chief Superintendent Rankin's hospitality at the Loup de Mer, an esoteric little restaurant nestling in the lee of the cathedral close.

'So my idea was a good one?' The Superintendent was wrestling with a plate of crayfish, his hands and chin running with the buttery sauce as he cracked and snapped his way through the pink shells to suck out the pulpy meat of their claws.

Proby, quite content with his dish of devilled whitebait, nodded gratefully. 'So far, so good.'

'I'm not sure about this blackmail scam. I don't think the Chief would approve.' Mr Rankin, who was unmarried, had no inhibitions about picking his teeth, using for the purpose a tiny gilt instrument which lived, when not in use, in a velvet pouch secured by a black pearl.

'Need he know?' The slim attentive waitress was refilling his glass with Chablis.

'Good heavens, no! Don't give him the whole bottle!' roared his host. 'Where's my ratatouille?' She scurried away.

'It's a bit of a risk,' Proby persisted.

'It's a good plan,' said the other. 'It might work.' He paused to drain his glass. 'You can't expect the sister to have to meet him face to face. If he is guilty, he's bound to try to kill her.'

'Precisely.'

'So?'

'We'll need a volunteer.'

'Here comes the ragout. You're going to enjoy this!' They turned their attention to the lamb.

'You want me to do *what*?' Julie, proudly wearing her sergeant's stripes, stared angrily at him. He was looking more like a bear than ever, a thick, confused, cantankerous bear with shaggy grey hair.

He stared back helplessly. He was exhausted and his head was throbbing with the aftermath of the Superintendent's dinner. He wasn't even officially back on the case. But the team were all there. And no one would question his authority, knowing he had Mr Rankin behind him. 'It's the only way.'

'The only way to get me killed!'

'We'll be there.'

'Oh, great! An audience! I'll just love dying in front of an audience. A bloody great hole in my belly, and you saying, "Well *done*, Julie." ... It's a great offer, I'm very flattered, *no thank you*!'

'He'll kill again. You have all got to understand, violence on this level is contagious, contaminating.'

'Well, it isn't going to be *me*, that's all I'm saying.'

'She's right,' said Rootham. 'It's a terrible risk. This isn't some half-baked villain stoned out of his tiny mind. This man is trained to kill.'

Julie turned on him. 'Who asked for your opinion? This is between Jim and me.' It was the first time she'd called Proby by his Christian name.

Rootham raised his hands in mock surrender. 'Sorry I spoke.'

'Tell me again,' she said to Proby. 'Tell me the plan.'

Encouraged by something in her expression, he leant forward. 'It's quite simple,' he said. 'Miss Beddoes has already made contact with him. You've all heard the tape. He's hooked, or damn near it.'

'So?'

'So – it's a thousand to one he'll try to kill her. What choice has he got? If this unknown woman really did see

165

him murder Beddoes, none of his smart friends would be able to save him. We might not be able to tag him with our murders, but he'd go down for life for that one. And life at his age means just about what it says. He's got to kill her.'

'Why would she meet him?'

'Because she's greedy, and stupid.'

'Why will he believe that?'

'Because she's an actress. She's playing the part of her life, a confused, venal, blackmailing spinster who doesn't recognize a sabre-toothed tiger when she sees one.'

'Except it's me he kills?'

'No,' he said patiently. 'It's you he tries to kill. We – ' he waved his hand expansively round the room, taking in the rows of rapt detectives – 'will protect you, and arrest him.' There was no doubt about the exultation in his voice.

'Where will the meeting take place?'

'She's going to specify a drop for the money. He'll stake it out, only we'll be there before him. You go and collect it. He pounces. We take him.'

'What if it's a bomb?'

He hadn't thought of that. He paused to consider the idea, then shook his head. 'That's not likely. It would create a new investigation. He's sure to stick to a shotgun, while creating an iron-clad alibi for himself. That way it will distance him further from my discredited suspicions. Nevertheless,' he added, making an extra note on his pad, 'we'll take precautions.'

'I want to be armed.'

'Of course. I've booked you in all afternoon, starting in – ' he consulted his watch – 'forty minutes. The armourer is expecting you. You'll also have some unobtrusive body armour.'

'Sounds like a picnic.' She smiled at him. Rootham looked glum. After all, their murderer had gone for head shots, every time.

*

'I wondered when you would call again.' Henry had spent much of the day testing his line. It had shown negative on all the regular tests to reveal any signs of surveillance.

'I've got my work to do, like anyone else,' said Mrs Brown, 'but now I've got time for you. You're lucky I kept quiet. And I've been thinking.'

'Yes?' he said. 'What about?'

'It wasn't you that did away with your wife?'

'No,' he said. 'I loved my wife.'

'Oh well,' she said. 'Too bad. Now about my mortgage.' He said nothing. 'My paper says you're big in some Ministry and you live at a posh address. So I reckon you could do it all in one lump.'

'How much?' He could see no point in prevaricating.

'Well...' He could almost hear her calculating how much she could ask for. 'It's £23,750.'

He almost laughed out loud at the modesty of her demand. 'I can't manage that,' he said automatically. To agree would be to invite immediate further demands. 'But I could give you £21,000 if I can be sure that will settle the matter.'

'Oh yes,' she said smugly. 'A deal's a deal.'

'Because if I do hear from you again, I'll have to kill you, won't I?' He was rewarded by a sharp intake of breath. 'Where shall I send the cheque?'

She laughed nervously. 'I don't want a cheque,' she said.

'Why on earth not?'

'Because then you could trace me.' Perhaps she wasn't quite as stupid as she sounded. 'I'd like it in cash. And not new notes neither. I'll ring you next week, to give you time to collect it. Then we'll arrange to meet.'

'Aren't you afraid I'll be accompanied by the police?' he asked.

She roared with laughter. 'Heavens no,' she said. 'I saw what you did, quite clearly. I'm not worried about that at all!' And rang off, leaving him far from satisfied.

Chapter 27

'Why the church in Brickyard Lane?' Proby, Rootham, Julie and a very subdued Miss Beddoes, brought up to Hampton under armed guard, were all sitting round the Superintendent's desk. He, nursing a poisoned finger from careless gardening, was studying Proby's provisional plan.

'Because we want him to feel he has a sporting chance, but there's no ground cover. The gravestones were all moved last year to suit the Council gardening department, and the yew avenue shown there was cut down for the same reason.'

'Very helpful!'

'Quite. He can't get in without our seeing him, and he certainly can't get out either.'

'If he kills me, you mean,' said Julie quietly. She had abandoned her pink lipstick for a translucent gloss, and had dark smudges under her eyes.

'By teatime tomorrow, it'll be over,' said Proby, lighting a cigarette from the stub of its predecessor. 'I'll be in the organ loft, Oates in the crypt, and Pirkis and Redvers will be in the vestry. He'll never even get the chance to fire. One move, and we'll have more than enough for a conviction.'

The Superintendent nodded. 'What about the poor congregation?'

'There won't be one.'

'What if he sees only one woman in church?'

'He's a Church of England church-warden,' put in Proby. 'He'll be used to small congregations. In any case, that's what he's expecting to see. She's explained she knows that the church is always unlocked, because her husband's a friend of the vicar.'

'Small world?'

'Better than trying to trap him in London. With all his contacts at Scotland Yard, someone would tip him off for certain. We ought to consider imposing radio silence on this. We don't want him picking up the plan on some fancy MOD machine.'

'He didn't sound surprised by the site,' mused Rootham. 'Where do you suppose he raised the money?'

'I don't expect he has,' said Proby. 'He's not going to pay her after all.'

'What if he does?'

'We'll all look a little stupid,' said Proby. 'But I've covered that with Travis of the Crown Prosecution Service. He'd be happy to proceed with that, though he'd rather he pulled a gun.'

'Well why doesn't he come and face this bleeding maniac instead of me?' cried Julie. 'If he's so fucking keen on shotguns, why doesn't he come and have a look down the barrels himself?'

Rankin stared at her angrily. He turned on Proby. 'I thought you told me this "officer" had volunteered?'

'I have volunteered, "sir",' she spat. 'It's just the waiting that's getting to me.'

'I think you're wonderful,' said Miss Beddoes. 'He gives me the creeps just hearing his voice on the telephone.'

'What time did you tell him to meet you?'

'Three o'clock, like Jim here said. He said he couldn't make it till three thirty. We hadn't planned for that, so I just agreed. But I said I couldn't wait any later, because of my train back to London. The main thing was to get it set up during daylight hours.'

'Is the delay a problem?'

'No.' Proby shook his head.

'How do you expect him to fix an alibi?'

'I don't much care. It won't be relevant.'

'Not if he doesn't get away again.'

Proby didn't answer.

Alone in his house that night, he found he couldn't sleep. What if it went wrong, and Julie was killed? Or a maverick church-goer got in the way? Or Henry managed to evade them after all? The one problem that did not disturb him was whether he was after the right man. Twice he lifted the receiver to ring Sheila's parents, twice he paused and then put the handset back unused. Once the telephone rang, but when he answered it, there was silence on the line. For hours he paced the house, sometimes checking if she had taken anything that might suggest a permanent exit, sometimes just seeking any distraction from his own thoughts. At three he surrendered, and settled down on the sofa to play a batch of old movies. Within five minutes, he was fast asleep. He was woken by the sound of the front door opening. Sheila, carrying a small suitcase, came into the room, her golden hair gloriously back-lit by the winter dawn.

'Good Lord!' she said. 'What are you doing there?'

'I couldn't sleep,' he said blearily. His eyelids felt stuck together, and his voice was hardly more than a growl.

'Shall I get you some coffee?'

'Please.' He didn't dare ask her where she had come from at, what, seven in the morning.

'I couldn't sleep either,' she said, coming back into the room with a steaming mug. 'Dad was unbearable, so I decided to up sticks and come straight home.' She handed him the mug, and kissed him. 'You need a shave.'

He laughed, an awkward croak. 'No doubt!'

She sat down beside him. 'I've missed you.'

'I've missed you too.' Why not admit the truth? She waited until he had drunk the scalding coffee, and then led him to their bed. He was too exhausted to demur, and then too driven by desire for her to think beyond their passion. Later, cradling her in his arms, he found himself gently kissing her sleeping face with grateful tenderness. She stirred, throwing her arm round his neck and pulling his head down between her breasts. She murmured something indistinct, but already he too was sleeping peacefully again.

All that morning, while Proby slept, the designated church was stealthily prepared for the afternoon ambush. A stark building, half a mile from the railway terminus, put up by the brick company for its workers in 1880, it was still surrounded by the shoddy little streets of cottages built round it for its captive congregation. The company had closed years ago, and the brickyard itself now hosted a fruit-packing factory. Most of the local inhabitants went to the modern Methodist chapel in the next street if they went anywhere to pray, but the church had resisted every effort by the Diocesan board to demolish it. Half a dozen resolute supporters and a parson old enough to have secured the freehold of his living had stood firm against the Archdeacon and his ball and chain.

By noon, everyone was in position except Proby. They had taken over two houses on each side, entering each one from the rear, the occupants astounded to find uniformed officers in body armour and carrying sten-guns coming across their gardens, and deeply offended to find their own movements summarily curtailed and confined to the back of their houses regardless of previous plans.

'Where the hell is Proby?' For the tenth time, Chief Superintendent Rankin, peering through binoculars in the attic of the vicarage, addressed this question to the unhappy Rootham. 'I wish we could have kept a tail on Bryant, whatever the Chief said. Where *is* Proby?'

'I don't know, sir. He said he'd be here by eleven.'

'Has anyone rung his home?'

'There's no reply.'

'Personal pager?'

'Apparently not switched on.'

'Well, send a car round.'

'Right.' Rootham went downstairs to the only telephone in the house, an old-fashioned instrument on the pantry wall. He passed the vicar on the stairs, a bent old man with a shrunken waxy face and thin strands of dyed orange hair plastered across his freckled scalp. The whole operation was being handled on land-lines, in case their man had access to the police frequencies, until they had seen him safely into the church. As Rootham reached the phone, he saw Proby hurrying through the back garden, his face dripping with perspiration despite the cold.

'Has he arrived?' Proby could hardly get the words out, he was panting so hard.

'No.' It was all Rootham could do to avoid looking at his watch. 'Everyone's in place.'

'Except me,' said Proby ruefully. 'I overslept and then the car wouldn't start. I've run most of the way.'

'You can't go in there now. He may turn up at any minute. When you didn't appear, I sent Braithwaite up to the organ loft with the Mannlicher. He won the Divisional Prize for shooting last year.'

'Well done. What's the forecast?'

'Light rain, possibly some fog this evening.'

'Lighting-up time?'

'Four twenty-five.' Rootham had known he would ask.

'Should be over by then. Where's Mr Rankin?'

'Upstairs with the vicar. Miserable old sod! He thinks it's all a plot by the Bishop to blow up his church.'

'Where's Julie?'

'She wanted to have a last-minute talk to you. I told her you were tied up. She's going to walk in there at 3.25. If she rings in again, I'll put her on.' They checked their watches: 12.17 p.m. More than three hours to wait.

Chapter 28

'So where is he?' Julie's voice had a metallic edge to it. She was ringing from a call-box three streets away, as they hadn't dared risk equipping anyone in the church with personal radios. Five powerful directional microphones had been drilled and wired into the pews, but even they would not be switched on until both parties to the fateful meeting were inside the building. With luck, their prey would have other things on his mind than continuing to check for electronic surveillance.

'I don't know,' said Proby dully. It was nearly twenty-five past three. Surely Henry would want to get there first? Could he be in there already? They had no means now of finding out. Had he been there already when they moved in? If so, surely he would have aborted. He had nothing to gain from coming out into the open once he knew the police were involved.

'I'm doing this for you,' she said.

'For me?' He rubbed his eyes. They kept closing.

'Yes,' she said sadly, sensing his lack of concentration. 'I've always been a bad picker.' And hung up.

'No sign of that rain,' remarked Rootham.

'No, but the fog's beginning to come in,' said Proby in a subdued voice. He hadn't anticipated Julie's declaration, and it had come as a considerable shock. Had he encouraged her? What a waste of her capacity to cherish someone free and young enough to hope. As for his wife . . .!

'What's wrong with your eyes?' The Chief Superintendent had come into the room. 'That daft bugger upstairs doesn't like my cigarettes.'

'He's out there somewhere,' said Proby. 'We ought to have had him tailed.'

'And have the Chief put us both back on the beat! Henry Bryant is a protected species as far as he's concerned. What *is* the matter with your eyes? You look as if you're crying.'

'Here she is!' They crammed as near to the window as they dared. Through the wisps of vapour, they could see Julie walking down the street towards the church. Twice she stopped and looked over her shoulder. They could only guess at her expression. She kept one hand firmly in her raincoat pocket.

'What's she carrying?'

'A Webley magnum. She could stop an elephant with that thing.'

'Where's the nearest man to her now?'

'Inside that heap of sacks by the wall. He's been there since last night. One of the SPG lads from Easingwold.'

'She's turning through the gate. Why didn't we give those men radio links inside?'

'You know damn well why,' snapped Rankin. 'Because if he's carrying one of those handy radio detectors, he'd just walk straight on past. You said so yourself!'

Proby shook his head anxiously. 'I'm not happy about this fog. We should have called it off when we heard the forecast.'

'Well, maybe we would have done,' hissed his exasperated superior, 'if you'd been around to offer that opinion this morning. This whole operation is your baby. Every man and woman out there is risking their lives because they trust and respect you. So wake up and get back to your usual form. What's up with you today? It's like being on duty with a zombie lookalike.'

It was true. He was only half alive. The abject surrender of his self-respect on the altar of mindless sexual appetite had almost unmanned him.

'If you're going to have a nervous breakdown,' Rankin added, 'wait till tomorrow, there's a good chap.'

'Coffee?' It was Rootham, an uncharacteristically tentative look on his face. 'It's good. Out of one of those machines. Methuselah sprinkled the chocolate on himself!'

Proby drank it gratefully, scalding his lips on the liquid beneath the froth. They stood and stared down the darkening street.

'He's not coming,' said Rankin at last. It was after four and the fog was beginning to form dense patches of smoky yellow gas which shone like sulphur in the glare of the yellow street lights. They had just come on, automatically illuminated by an unseen hand.

'She's coming out.' Rankin pointed at the slim white figure hurrying down towards the wych-gate.

'I don't blame her,' said Rootham. 'She's had enough for one day.'

'But that's what he wants,' shouted Proby, shocking them with his sudden violence. 'He never was going to meet her. He's waiting out there to kill her on the way to her train.'

'Which . . .'

Proby was already flying down the stairs, taking them three at a time.

'Give me that!' He snatched the revolver out of the hands of a startled constable crouching behind the front door, and was out in the street before the man could protest. Julie was already out of sight, three hundred yards up the street and lost in the mist. He could just hear her footsteps, clattering on the frosty pavement. A man rose out of the shadows.

'It's me, you fool!' hissed Proby, ignoring the threatening automatic. 'Follow me, and keep quiet.' Together they raced up the street, running, yet so delicately that it was more like the lope of an antelope than the pace of an athlete.

Less than two hundred yards away now, Julie was striding ahead, tears streaming down her face. She had waited

175

and waited in the church. Bloody Jim Proby hadn't even fucking well turned up to protect her from the gallery. She had risked her life for a man who couldn't understand and didn't care. A married man at that! She wiped her eyes, and gave a little shriek. A thin pale figure had stepped smartly out of the swirling mist and was pointing a shotgun straight at her.

'Mrs Smith, I presume?'

'Mrs 'Oo?' She exaggerated her accent, striving for something to distract him. At least Jim had been right. It was unmistakably Henry Bryant behind the absurd stage moustache. She groped for her gun, saw the movement in his eyes, and flung herself despairingly to her left as he fired. The impact of the shot took her by surprise, hurling her against the wall behind. Time seemed suspended, she heard two more shots and saw dark stains spreading across his white coat. He fired again into the fog and dimly she heard someone scream. She managed to raise her own gun, but then he was gone, a wraith among so many others, a shadow melting into the mist.

'Are you okay?' Rootham was leaning over her.

'I wasn't holding my gun,' she murmured. 'The Armourer *told* me never to leave go of it.'

'Jim's gone after him,' he said, laying his coat over her, to hide the terrible wound. 'Here's Braithwaite. The ambulance is on its way.'

Following the sound of his quarry's pounding feet through the freezing swirls of mist, Proby hardly noticed the growing pain in his chest, as each panting breath seared through his body. Far ahead of him he heard the angry snarl of a diesel engine bursting into life, and he threw himself into a doorway as a small van bucketed over the pavement before careering off down the street. He caught just a glimpse of Henry, his bloodless face half-hidden under a floppy woman's hat, crouched over the wheel. The street was completely empty. He pounded after the van, which rounded the corner narrowly missing a small car which veered into some dustbins. The driver was still sitting in his seat, staring at the debris, when Proby reached him.

'Quick,' he said, pulling open the door. 'Get out! Police!'

'Shove off,' growled the man, his eyes fuddled with drink. 'What about that other bugger?'

Proby stuck his revolver in the man's face. 'Move!' he said. The man sprawled across the seat and threw himself out of the other door, rolling on to the mess of refuse. Reversing into the road, Proby sent the car spinning round and accelerating in the direction Henry had taken. Where would he head? Certainly not home, since he would be expected there. No one had seen him except Julie. If she died, and from the look of her as Proby had run past, she well might, the only new evidence against Henry would be if their shots had hit him. If he was unharmed, he had only to evade immediate capture now to remain, if not safe, at least with a reasonable chance of acquittal in the event of a trial. He decided to take the northern ring road. As soon as he reached the outer suburbs away from the estuary, the fog died away, revealing a stormy January evening, with spots of rain blown across his screen by the wind. He took the spur road on to the Carlton road and was rewarded by the sight of some lights half a mile ahead. Whatever the vehicle was, it turned off towards Claxby. On an impulse Proby followed, still closing the gap, and within two minutes he was right behind the same delivery van that had nearly crushed him earlier. Henry must have seen something in his mirror, for the van suddenly leapt forward and took another sudden turn up a concealed lane, leaving Proby to brake on the main road and reverse before following the new route in pursuit.

He's heading for the woods, Proby thought. There was no sign of the van. Angrily, he stopped and peered around in the gathering dusk. The main woods were up a salient on his left, with more forestry away to the right. Which way to go? Suddenly he saw a flicker of light. Then

177

another. It was about half a mile away, among some tall conifers. He drove as near as he could, bumping the car across some sticky plough until the wheels would turn no further. Then, checking that he had four bullets left in the revolver, he started to run heavily towards the light, the heavy clay clutching at his shoes. By the time he reached it, the little van was blazing cheerfully, its whole interior seething with red and orange flames. Without pausing, he plunged into the trees.

Somewhere a twig snapped. The wind had got up, and twice he was startled by the suddenly flapping wings of a pigeon sideslipping out of the gale, only to change its mind on sensing his presence. All around him the trees stretched away, sightless witnesses to centuries of primitive life and death. The ceaseless cycle of nature had never seemed to him so emphatic in its brooding presence. This time he definitely heard a footstep. He turned. The trees presented bare innocent faces and the leafless branches waved as if in surrender as the wind whistled painfully through the cracks in their bark. Another step! What was he doing here among these faceless phantoms, pursuing an armed quarry without support? Suddenly he was afraid. Was this the true meaning of panic, this shuddering palpitating fear, this sense of the occult, of present evil? Two large liquid eyes watched him from behind a clump of brambles, followed him as he took a few more steps, then paused, as if conscious of their scrutiny, and turned. He saw the eyes, opened his mouth and then almost laughed aloud with relief as the brown hare spun on its haunches and scampered away into the pine thicket.

'I'm glad it's you.' Henry was almost beside him, propped up against a tree, with a shotgun levelled at Proby's chest.

'You'd better give me that.'

Henry laughed, precipitating a thin pale dribble of blood from the side of his mouth. 'Give me a minute,' he said. 'Drop your gun.'

'It's over.'

'Move your hand just half an inch, and it'll be well and truly over for you. I don't know who trains you people. It's been like playing in the nursery.' The whole of his coat front was soaked with blood, but his eyes were alert, amused. 'Drop that gun!'

Having no choice, Proby obeyed. 'Why did you do it?'

'I want to talk about your wife. What she did to me. What she liked me doing to her.' Henry was having to shout above the shriek of the wind.

Proby shrugged. 'Give me the gun and you can talk about anything you like.' The hurricane was screaming now, the branches signalling fantastic semaphores before the gale.

Henry's mouth was wide open, shouting now in exultation above the wailing storm, 'I've fucked your wife, and now I'm going to kill you! Happy New Year, Jim!' The wind had risen to a colossal blast, and the jagged black hole that appeared abruptly in what had been Henry's face drenched blood and brains all over Proby's outstretched arms. The crack of the rifle-shot echoed a moment later, ricocheting off the wooden sentinels around them. Henry's body, nothing now but a lifeless trunk, sank first to its knees and then subsided on to the sodden ground. The fingers of his left hand twitched and contracted among the pine needles, then stretched out in a final vibrating spasm, and became still.

'Not bad for eighty yards.' Clark, the gamekeeper, turned Henry's body over with the heel of his boot. 'Bloody vermin! Have a swig of this.' He passed Proby a hip-flask which the shaken policeman put unsteadily to his lips.

'Thanks,' he said.

The gamekeeper shrugged his shoulders. 'I like to be out in the woods on nights like these. Isn't that sky beautiful?' They looked up at the vast clouds fleeing across the dark sky, feeling their faces spattered by the rain. 'I always knew it was him, the bastard!' He kicked the body again.

Soon people would come to collect Henry's body. Soon

he would learn whether Julie had survived. He would have to face the Chief Constable, the press, his wife. But just for the moment, he was happy to feel the wind in his face, to taste the gamekeeper's whisky searing his throat. He leant back against a tree trunk, and closed his eyes.

Chapter 29

'He really tried to kill you?'

'He certainly did his best!' Proby was stretched out on the sofa at home, nursing an undiluted glass of whisky. Occasionally he sipped it, enjoying the sting of the liquid as it ran down the back of his throat.

'And he killed all those other women?' She still couldn't really believe it.

'I've told you,' he said, smiling patiently. 'It was a cover for killing Anne. Elaborate, but potentially successful. Once he'd decided to kill Anne, he had to kill the others first, to forestall an overwhelming suspicion falling on him, were Anne the first or only victim.' Now it was all over, Proby felt nothing but protective sympathy for his wife. 'He thought she was betraying him by having an affair.' Their eyes met for the briefest of seconds.

'And was she?'

'I don't know, but I don't think so. Nor did he at the end. He reckoned he'd made a mistake.'

'You men!' She was crouched on the floor, wearing her green silk wrap and leaning heavily against his side, one hand idly caressing his chest. 'You're so possessive.'

'Possessiveness comes from weakness,' he said.

'Or pride.'

'Pride is a weakness,' he replied. 'And not to be confused with self-respect.'

'And you?' she blurted. 'Doesn't *my* stupidity dent your self-respect?' She wasn't looking at him now, but studying some blemish on her hand.

'Why should it? It may dent yours, but I regard you as an individual, not as a chattel.'

She turned her pale blue gaze full upon him. 'I can't decide,' she said slowly, 'if that shows great generosity or great arrogance!'

He shrugged and drank deeply, gasping at the liquor's fiery passage. 'I'm a policeman, not a psychiatrist.'

'I still don't understand. What made you so certain it was him?'

'The missing brooch.'

'What missing brooch?' He could tell her attention was wandering.

'It's not important. We're trained to look for inconsistencies. They're a sight easier to find than fingerprints. And in some ways just as conclusive. There was a regimental brooch which was in our original inventory of Anne's presents to Henry. Later he hid it because he knew it was incriminating. I knew then for certain that he was our man. And what was more important, so did he. Being in the same business gave him an edge at the start, but it made him more aware of his danger at the end. And once he knew we'd fingered him for real, he was very vulnerable to the threat of hard evidence. He was deputy head of counter-terrorism, you know, that's why there was nothing about him on the computer. Officially, he hardly existed!'

'So why did he hide the brooch?'

'Who knows? Perhaps it was a symbol of what he saw as his wife's infidelity? Perhaps its purchase was in some way significant? Perhaps it could lead us to his past. We know that she bought it with her friend. Maybe Henry didn't realize until he unwrapped those presents after he'd killed her that the brooch was actually for him. We'll never know now.'

'And me? Did he use me just to get at you?'

'Of course not!' He smiled reassuringly down at her. 'He had no reason to know I would be in charge of the case. I'm sure he loved you.'

182

She shook her head. 'No,' she said. 'He certainly didn't love me. He wanted a woman. I happened to be there. It was just sex.'

'And you?' He didn't want an answer, but there seemed no way to avoid the question.

She stared at him, her eyes filling with tears. Her gown had fallen open, revealing her breasts. 'I can't explain. Not even to myself. What shall we do now?' He put down his glass on the carpet beside her, and ran a speculative finger over her body. 'Is that what you want?' She was smiling now, though whether from relief or from anticipation would have been hard to say.

'Yes.' And there was a savage intensity to his lovemaking, a celebration of dominance and of being alive which took her by surprise. Nor was its violence altogether unwelcome to her. If he had never been so demanding, she had never been so softly submissive. There was something almost sacrificial in her yielding acquiescence. He was still lying heavily across her, half-dozing despite the glare of the overhead light, when the telephone began its insistent interruption. It was Rootham, reporting that Julie had come through a four-hour operation, and the prognosis was cautiously optimistic.

'She kept calling for you.'

Proby's face showed nothing beyond polite interest. 'Who's staying with her?'

'Mr Rankin. Can I say you'll look in later?'

'No. I'll be over first thing in the morning, before I start on the report. You'd better get some sleep yourself.'

'There's been a knifing over at Tino's. And Traffic say more snow is forecast. They're worried about the Royal visit to Britoil.'

'I'll worry about that in the morning. Get some rest.'

'You too.'

He looked across the room at the pale fleshy buttocks of his wife, as she sprawled on the cushions, with a dark shadow running down one side of her belly, her head hidden by the angle at which she lay. Sometimes it was difficult to tell the difference between life and death. For all the movement there, she might have been one of Henry's victims. But it was over, his wife was alive, was his, and tomorrow, no doubt, he would have a new case.